ISABEL'S SKIN

ALMA BOOKS LTD
London House
243–253 Lower Mortlake Road
Richmond
Surrey TW9 2LL
United Kingdom
www.almabooks.com

First published by Alma Books Limited in 2012
Copyright © Peter Benson, 2012

Peter Benson asserts his moral right to be identified as the author of this
work in accordance with the Copyright, Designs and Patents Act 1988

Printed in England by CPI Group (UK) Ltd, Croydon, CR0 4YY

Typeset by Tetragon

ISBN: 978-1-84688-206-7

ISABEL'S SKIN

PETER BENSON

ALMA BOOKS

Other books by PETER BENSON
published by Alma Books

The Levels

A Lesser Dependency

The Other Occupant

Odo's Hanging

Riptide

A Private Moon

The Shape of Clouds

Two Cows and a Vanful of Smoke

ISABEL'S SKIN

We shall not all sleep, but we shall all be changed.

1 Corinthians 15:51

Prologue

I wrote this story in a wooden house at the bottom of a thin garden. Turn your back on the sea, cross the lawn, walk past the bushes, the flower beds and the pond with the statue of a dog. Stop, take a deep breath and look.

The house was built to face south-east. Climb five steps, watch out for the loose board, cross a veranda, open the front door and there you are, standing with the light coming in and the sound of birds in the marshes.

The house has a bedroom at the back, a sitting room and kitchen in the front, and a small bathroom at the side. It is built of cedar planks with a felted pitched roof, two windows at the front, the door in the middle, two windows in the sides and one in the back.

The air smells of apples, wax paper, a collection of pinned beetles and dust. These smells collect and concentrate and turn in the air, like leaves drifting through an autumn wood. There are memories in the air too, of spilt drinks and candles burning through the night, and lost days. I say the place has memories, and these are some of the memories I imagine it has, but I do not know. I cannot tell what is hidden in the walls and floors, or what the windows have seen. I know what I have seen and will tell you about the places I have been, and how they have brought me to this place and state, but that is all I will tell you. There are some things I like to be private about, and I will be.

I have good, solid furniture, carpets and rugs, pictures of ships in rough seas and a stove in the corner of the drawing room. There is a table in the kitchen and in a cupboard a telescope that does not work. Three chairs that do not match, a salt cellar and a note on the wall that reads "Please close down the stove before leaving". A pair of cracked plates, some white pebbles we found on the beach and puddles of hard wax on the sill. All the curtains have shrunk, so there is a gap around the bottom of the windows.

At the back of the house is a low barn with stables for two horses, and a shed filled with old tools, lengths of wood and boxes. A water butt stands by the shed, and a lean-to with room for cut logs.

When the wind blows the house moans, and when the sun shines it creaks, and when it rains it sighs like it wants the rain so much, and now here it is and here I am, listening all the time. I listen for a whimper and a cry, but I know it will not come. I know I wait in vain. I wait in vain, but will not be defeated.

In the old days, my father used to allow members of the clergy to use this place for their holidays, but I do not. Since he left it to me, I keep strangers away. The clergymen go somewhere else, but I do not know where. They have their own lives and travels, and I have nothing to do with them.

Now I have finished writing this story I must get away and do something I have never done before. With this in mind, I started to read a book about a man who travelled through the greater part of Asia to Siam, where he met the King and learnt to fight monkeys. He was an old man and he always wore a hat. He had survived snake bites as a child and grew up to become an important cartographer. I read the first page and most of the second. The man was standing outside a hotel in Glasgow, he had lost his pen and it was pouring with freezing rain. He was soaked to the skin and wrote a page about the terrible weather and how philosophers would never understand the true meaning of misery. I did not read any more of that book.

I did not read any more because here you can sit at the kitchen table, dab your fingers in a pool of spilt milk and look out at the marshes. You can hear the bitterns boom, the knifed birds of the reeds, perfect for the place, mad and vengeful, never forgetting a slight. Or you can lie in bed and not read a book and listen to the curlews, or you can walk up the garden path, through the gate, across the road and into the marshes.

The marshes whisper and the marshes cry and the marshes threaten. They are like someone you like but cannot trust. They never look you in the eye and they never buy a drink. They whisper behind their hands and walk with a sly smile. If you leave the paths, the ground will look safe but will lead into a swamp, and you will slip and fall and either spend your last night on earth face down in water or face up, and birds will eat your eyes. Some people say, "The marshes are so beautiful and lonely" – and they are right, but they do not know the whole story. It is too easy to say those sort of things about a place, as though beauty can hide a grave.

So this is my house at the edge of the marshes with its roof, floors and chairs, and there go a flock of geese, and this is my house too. It is like everyone's other house, a place where secrets, promises, dreams and terrors are kept. Mine is like this.

It is not a lasting state, this house, but it changes every day. It holds things that never leave – the memory of the first time I saw her, the sound of her cries echoing in the night, the smell of her sweat, the feel of her – and it grows, twists and adds things to itself.

It could be mad or it could be angry, or it could double back on itself and become taller than the tallest building in a city you visited once and wish you could see again. It could be yellow and black and talk in a language only it understands. It could whisper about careless times, or flare like a candle and become the person you loved, someone who took your life and wrenched it away. Her name could chime, and when you are so lonely and you pull her image from an envelope and stare at it in the middle of the night you know she was the love of your life and you will never forget her. You can smell her skin, the skin that hurt so much, but then the smell passes. It has gone, and before you have a chance, you find yourself screaming in the night and wailing into the day.

It is as bad as that, as bad as the grave-digger who thinks, for a second, about what would happen if the man at the top walked away and left him there with his spade and his bucket and the block of light shining down. Or it could be a pale sky with me walking along, and skylarks are watering the air with their songs. The sky is the roof and the larks are bees in the rafters, and I wake in the middle of the night from a dream about being a more dangerous man than I am.

I sit up, and as the wind plays with the marshes, I remember how her skin used to ripple like water under ice. I used to lean towards her, put my ear next to her nose and listen to her breathing. I used to do these things, but now I sit and wait and watch the wind in the marshes, and dust balls roll around my feet.

I wait and wait, and as the night dies I lie down and fall asleep again and drift through dreams about rare books burning and syringes. But I am not disturbed. I take these things and sweep them into the corner of my head I keep away from. It is exactly like this, and I do not wonder why.

And I remember she was wailing about ants under her skin, and when I tried to hold her she screamed, beat me off and then held on to me. Her shoulder blades were like wings folded beneath her poor skin, and I thought all I had to do was take a knife and release those wings and she would have freedom. I could have folded the flaps of skin, and feathers could have grown from her blood, like her blood was magic and I had a greater power. Her bones might have clicked and spread and sung along their edges, and my knife could have sung in return, but it did not.

I ran my fingers over those hidden wings and kissed the back of her neck. She twitched and buried her head in the pillow. She blinked and her eyes filled with tears, but she did not have to say anything. She did not have to say anything at all. She was quiet and then she was still and there was nothing I could do. I was not lost when I found her, but I had no idea where I was.

Somerset

I used to be a book valuer. I was employed by an auction house. I was trusted, respected and pleased. I lived in London in comfortable rooms, and I had money in the bank. I lived alone, and although I had friends and acquaintances, I was not close to any of them. I had brown hair and blue eyes.

Most mornings I stirred at seven and lay awake for five minutes, then got up from my bed, washed and drank a cup of tea in my kitchen. I stared at the tree in the garden next door. It was a horse chestnut, a tall, old and beautiful tree. I used to stare at it while I ate two slices of toasted bread and marmalade. I ate two slices and always spread the same sort of marmalade. It was very bitter and made the tea taste delicious. My rooms were on the top floor of a house close by Highbury Fields. Beyond, to the north and west, spread the swelling slums of the city and their cloaks and dresses of smoke and filth. I did not know these places, and I tried to keep them at a distance. I confess my ignorance, though my ignorance was not bred of disinterest. I believed the ragged should live in the minds of the fortunate, but I was still – and thought I would always be – a top-floor man.

I dressed smartly in a black suit, white shirt and a plain tie, a fine bowler, polished brogues, and I carried a black-leather briefcase. I left my rooms at eight, bought *The Times* from a kiosk on the corner of my street, and caught an omnibus to work. I read the letters page and the theatre reviews, and watched my fellow passengers, the buildings we passed and the traffic.

Most days I spent at a desk in a fine building on the Strand. I had a wide, polished desk and a view of the Thames. I loved the stinking river, the swell, the current, the barges and lighters, the wash of the tide against the walls, the colour and the promise of leaving. I loved the way the water gave the daylight life, and the way the night lights spun and reflected. Nothing remained the same. The river never slept.

My office was large and comfortable, the walls were lined with books and catalogues, and there were a few pictures in the gaps between the shelves. A pleasant watercolour of the Norfolk coast, a brush-and-ink painting of a sleeping cat, an engraving of a vicious bittern stalking its rival through the reeds, a reproduction of a sailing yacht cutting through a rough sea. My chair was leather and I always used black ink. Always black ink and a thin nib. I suppose I lived the life of an average bachelor, settled into what I thought was comfort, inured to the city, dreaming of something else but not sure what, lost in work and habits and the conventions that cloaked my work.

* * *

As I said, in those days I spent most of my time in London, but sometimes I was asked to break my routine and leave the city, travel to the shires and provinces, risk my tracts and stomach, drink different beer, sleep in yellow bedrooms owned by women called Mrs Lloyd or Mrs MacTavish, and eat breakfasts of huge eggs, fried bread, pork sausages and red bacon. I would be obliged to talk to insane men, or wonder about women with black eyes. There would be roads to travel, and boats to dream of. There were libraries to look at, collections to value and individual volumes to examine. One week I could be in Northumberland, the next in Inverness, maybe a month later in Sussex. Then an old house in Wales or Cheshire, or a place in Cornwall. I could never tell. I am not psychic. I am a small man. No. In my shoes, I am big enough.

So, last year I was asked to travel to Somerset to value the collection of the late Lord Malcolm Buff-Orpington, who had spent half a lifetime collecting original editions by authors of the French Enlightenment. Why the authors of the French Enlightenment? I did not know, was not told and never found out, but collectors are like this; they have an obscure idea that grows, for no obvious reason, into something that takes on a life of its own, spreading, binding, obsessing and then trapping. And so it was with Buff-Orpington, whose original plan had been to assemble all the English editions of Voltaire published in the eighteenth century. But over the years this plan grew, and by the time of his death the Buff-Orpington collection was one of the finest of its kind and included first and second editions and pamphlets by Voltaire, Rousseau, Diderot and the others.

I had a vague idea why the family were selling the collection – something to do with an irrational dislike the new Lord Buff-Orpington had for all things French – but this had nothing to do with me. The auction house had important clients waiting for my valuation, and as I left London I could smell the pages, feel the marbled covers and chipped corners and see the light foxing. I could hear the sound of old words rustling in their paragraphs and the blink of carefully placed punctuation. A complete nine-volume set of Œuvres, published in Dresden in 1748 under Voltaire's personal supervision, had recently realized a surprising amount. If the rumours were true, the Buff-Orpington Œuvres were as close to mint as they could be.

I suppose – in those days I supposed and wondered and considered a great deal – I should have been excited, but I left London with a sense of trepidation. I always left London with a sense of trepidation, a worry that now my routine was disturbed I would not be able to sleep properly, or I would have trouble washing. Or I would not be able to find decent bread, or get lost, or I would be unable to get my clothes laundered. So I packed more than I needed – enough for three weeks, although I was only expecting to be away for ten days – and I took my own jar of marmalade.

I rode the railway from Paddington Station to Taunton. When I first told my father I was a regular passenger on the railways, he shook his head and said he would never be persuaded to travel faster than a horse could pull a dogcart. My father is retired now, but he used to be a parson in Dover. He used to believe mashed potato was dangerous, and when I was a child he used to frighten me with his talks, his livered hands and his huge eyebrows, and the sound of his footsteps in the corridor, but those days have passed now. Days come and days pass, and it is too easy to think you know what happened. People change and you think you knew who they were, who you were and how you reached the place you find yourself in, but you know nothing. You know nothing at all, and anyone who tells you they have found the truth has only found their truth, nothing more. As people who think they have found the truth always end up raving, foaming and talking to plain walls, so people who allow their lives to die in routine only see the edge of the world. But I do not know; sometimes I wish I could go back and meet Michel Eyquem, Seigneur de Montaigne, and we could sit together on a broad terrace with a view of his estate and I could ask him if he thought anything I said or thought or wrote had any merit. But maybe not. As the great man said, "I may have read widely, but I cannot remember a thing."

I almost enjoyed the journey, rattling out of the city, through the smoke and dirt, past the filthy houses and cottages that seemed to wish themselves closer to the tracks, leaving the dust heaps and chocked streets behind. I allowed myself to enjoy a disturbed nap until we reached the first fields and the engine began to trundle at a regular speed, and then we were

quickly at the business of alarming horses and frightening
birds from the trees. A recent report had blamed a spark from
a railway train for a fire that destroyed five acres of fine barley
outside Woking, and as we passed through one particularly
beautiful field, I saw a farmer standing by a gate, his stick
raised in fury, his face red, his pinched daughters standing
beside him like a posy.

More than anything, I think I enjoyed the cool air. Since
May, London's smog had been particularly thick, and the
summer's damp heat had not helped matters. There had
been days when I had been forced to hold a handkerchief to
my face as I walked the last few yards to my office. Now, as
we rode through Wiltshire, I lowered the carriage window a
few inches and allowed the smutted air to wash through the
compartment in the hope that I would be able to breathe
some fresh. I did not, so I closed the window, sat back and
dozed again.

We reached Taunton in the middle of the afternoon. I
left the train and bought a meat pie, and after a pointlessly
discursive argument with a number of drivers, managed to
secure the services of a man who was prepared to carry me
the twenty or so miles to Buff-Orpington's home, Belmont
Hall, outside the village of Ashbrittle.

"It's a fair way," he said, patting his horse, "and there's
hills he'll have to climb."

"Get me there before nightfall and I'll make it worth your
while." I gave him a wide, gay smile, and patted my jacket
pocket.

The man shrugged, took my case, threw it up, and with a crack of his whip we were off, down the hill from the station, through the streets of the old town, a bustling market and onto the main road.

We drove for an hour or more before turning north and climbing into a dripping, saturated landscape. The country parishes of the west had been suffering the torments of a seemingly endless wet season, and as liver rot had decimated the sheep flocks, now foot-and-mouth disease was added to the farmers' woes. Here and there we saw a scowling man standing beside his emaciated, shivering cattle, but mostly the fields were empty, the barns echoing, the houses unloved and desperate. The cart rattled through the ruts and puddles, the horse panted, the driver cursed, the lanes narrowed, the hedges grew taller and the sky lower. As we climbed one hill and then another and dropped into a wooded valley, the sodden land seemed to open its arms to me, then slowly closed them. It folded and held me, bubbled in my ear, and my throat constricted. The valley was crowded with trees and a swollen stream followed the road. Clouds of sluggish insects swirled over the verges, and when the road began to climb again, the trees thinned out and a pair of buzzards appeared, drifting in circles over the fields and woods. I heard their cries over the hooves and the rattle of the wheels, and turned to watch them climb and fade into the watery horizon.

I had a map of the route to Buff-Orpington's house, but by the time we reached the hamlet of Appley we were lost. This place was no more than a couple of farms, a cluster of ruined houses and a public house. We stopped, and while the driver grumbled about the time and went to draw a bucket of water for the horse, I stepped down to stretch my legs. I stood under a tree and took a deep breath and thought, for a moment, that the peace was solid, like I could cut a piece of it and put it in my pocket.

I looked at the map, and as I was tracing our route from the main road and trying to establish where I had taken a wrong turn, the landlady came out, looked me up and down and opened her mouth to say something, but nothing came out. She was big and florid, with soiled bandages around her ankles and watery grey eyes. An old dog followed her and sniffed my shoes. I said, "Good afternoon" – and after a long pause she said, "So, you's lost then?"

"Yes," I said. "I think I am."

She gave me the ghost of a smile. "Where you heading to?" Her accent was hard and thick, like stones were rattling in her mouth.

I pointed on the map. "Belmont Hall. Ashbrittle."

"Ah," she said. "Belmont…" She let the word hang in the air. "Belmont. Poor Lord Malcolm. He were a fine gentleman." She tipped her head and waited for me to give a reason for wanting to visit the dead man's house, but I said nothing. She huffed and puffed and her dog wheezed.

"I think we took a wrong turn back there," and I pointed the way we had come.

"Yes," she said, "you did. You should have been going straight on."

"I thought so," I said.

"It's easy," she said, "to get lost in these parts. Too easy for strangers. Especially if you're going to Ashbrittle." She flashed me a look that snagged itself between pity and threat, and her dog gave a half-hearted bark. "Where you coming from?"

"London."

"From London? You come from London?"

"Yes, madam, I have."

"That's a busy town."

"It is."

"Too busy for me." She shook her head.

"Is it?"

"Yes. Busy, smelly, filthy. I wouldn't be going there if you paid me."

"I see," I said, and I was going to ask her if she had anything polite to say about the great city, but did not bother. She had a dangerous glint in her eyes, so I said "Maybe I'll have a drink" instead.

"A drink?" she said, and she managed a half-laugh.

"Yes," I said.

She gave me another of her smiles and said, "We're closed."

"Closed?" I could see a couple of people inside, drinking and looking at the floor. I took out my watch and checked the time. It was half-past seven.

"Yes," she said, "closed." And when I looked at her I knew there was no point arguing. Her eyes had turned to pinholes and her dog managed a snarl before turning around and staggering back to the pub.

"That's a great shame." I waited for her to laugh, but all she did was shake her head and give me a pitiful stare.

I returned to my driver. As I approached, he reached up, took down my bag, put it on the ground and said, "This is as far as I go." He looked at the sky. It was threatening rain. "I have to be home before nightfall."

"I beg your pardon?"

"I think you heard me."

"But it's only two more miles."

"Is it?"

"Yes."

"If it's only two more miles, you can walk."

"Walk?"

"Yes," said the driver, and now he pulled himself up to his full height, and I decided it was probably not wise to continue the argument. I reached into my jacket, took out my wallet and paid him the agreed sum, but withheld the extra I had promised. For a moment, I thought the argument was about to recommence, but he simply turned, climbed into his seat, whipped the horse and drove back the way we had come. Then I was left alone with the scowling landlady at my back, a puddled road ahead and the thick, heavy scents of the closing summer evening all around.

I had no choice, so I started to walk. I was not dressed for it – my city suit was hot, my bag was heavy, my shoes were unsuitable and the road soon became little more than a track – but I remembered something my father had once said: "The way may be strewn with difficulties, but your reward will be in the Lord." And as I trudged, I put myself in mind of the more unfortunate members of our society, men and women and children who have no choice but to tramp the highways and byways with nothing but hope and prayer. I had work and doubt – which, I supposed, was enough, and certainly more than whatever was possessed by the urchin who jumped out of the hedge opposite a tumbled-down smithy and chose to walk with me.

"You travelling?" he said.

"Yes," I said.

"Where you headin'?"

"Ashbrittle. Belmont Hall."

"Ashbrittle?" he said, and he whistled through his teeth, as though I was a brave man to be visiting such a place.

"You know it?"

"Oh yes," he said, "but I don't go there. Wouldn't go there. Not like it is."

"What do you mean?"

"There's bad things there."

"Bad things? What do you mean?"

He shook his head, looked at his black, calloused feet and hitched up his trousers. "Ma says there's bad things in Ashbrittle. Crawling things. Evil, she says."

"Evil? What sort of evil?"

"The screaming kind," he said. "Ma says you can hear her in the night time. Sometimes in the day too."

"Her?"

"Oh yes."

"A lady?"

The urchin looked this way and that, and a sudden frightened look crept into his eyes. He nodded. "I don't think she's a lady."

"Then who is she?"

"Might be a witch, might be a devil. I don't know. Don't care to, either."

"Have you seen her?"

"Oh no, not me. But my brother, he saw her."

"Did he?"

The boy nodded. "Oh yes. Saw her at her window. Said he'd never seen anything so frightening, and if Roger says he was frightened, he's not lying. My brother, he's a believer, and said, well, said she's bound to be bad. Bound to be walking with the devil. She had eyes like coals."

"And are you bad?" I said.

"Sometimes. Sometimes Ma says I'm worse than bad, but I don't know what that would be. But I couldn't be as bad as she…"

"Well," I said, as I crossed a bridge over a river, "all boys are worse than bad sometimes," but I don't think he heard me, because he wouldn't follow me over the bridge.

"Can't go any further," he said. "Got to go this way," and he pointed up the river bank.

"Why's that?" I said.

"Cos," he said, and he shrugged, and before I had the opportunity to question him further, he had hopped into the hedge and, with a whoop, disappeared into the fields.

I suppose – given how events unfolded – I should have listened carefully to the urchin. I should not have crossed that bridge and walked the final mile and a half. I should have turned around and returned to London, and I would have avoided the pain and death. I would not have got caught up in the horrors that waited for me, I would have remained the pleased top-floor man with a morning newspaper and simple, regular habits. But I was not a man who listened to gossip, rumour or threat, or the mild imaginings of hedge boys. Even when I was a child, even though I had a fill of the usual young terrors of the young, I refused to be frightened into a corner. My father used to tell me how God was always watching, taking note of my behaviour, logging it in a ledger that would be read at Judgement Day. And the severity of my sins would match the pain of the pins God's angels would use to pierce my flesh. Nonsense, I thought. If God was all-knowing, why would he need a ledger? He would remember. And if God loved the world, why did he allow a man to play as a small God with a beautiful woman like Isabel Carter? How could this happen? But stop. I am allowing a rush of anger to spill over the edge of this story. And I am getting ahead of myself.

Ashbrittle looked exhausted, almost dead, a stranded place. It stood at the top of a hill, and as I crossed its threshold, my first thought was one of dismay. For here the full force of the country parishes' desperation was displayed. The houses and cottages were in a ruinous and parlous state. Their roofs were holed and their walls unpainted, and the few crops in the kitchen gardens were in an advanced state of rot. Thin, ragged children stood in listless groups to watch me pass, until their mothers rushed from their hovels to pull them indoors. A group of labourers stood by the lychgate, their faces fierce and hollow, rusted tools stacked beside them. A broken cart was standing by a tumbled-down wall, an emaciated horse beside it. A pyre was burning somewhere, and as clots of filthy, evil-smelling smoke drifted over the village, I was forced to hold my handkerchief to my face and take deep, retching breaths.

I nodded to the men as I passed, and as two of them spat in my direction, I walked to the wall that ran around the churchyard, sat down and surveyed my map. Belmont Hall was marked with a cross at the end of a drive beyond the church, and as I was orientating myself, a man with a hoe poked his head over a garden wall, looked at the sky and said, "When's him going to stop?"

I said, "I'm sorry?"

"The rain. It's been too long." He had a huge head and red hair. His nose was twice the size it should have been and pitted like a walnut. He said, "You come to see the yew?"

"Yes I have. Amongst other things." I'd read about the famous Ashbrittle yew. It was ancient, and some claimed it was a thousand years old when Christ was born.

"Other things?"

The man squinted at me, so I gave him an explanation, and although I did not say anything about rare books, I did say I had an appointment at Belmont House.

"Belmont?"

"Yes."

"Then you'll be expected," said the man.

"I think I am."

The man nodded. "We never saw much of Lord Malcolm, but he were a gentleman, that's right. Rode an old nag. You'd think a man like that would ride something better, but no. Not at all. Took a tumble a year or two back. They said it were all over the papers."

"Was it?"

"They said so." The man shook his head. "After that, we saw even less of him. Used to see the housekeeper."

"Is that Miss Watson?"

"Yes. She were devoted."

"Was she?" I said, and I looked at my watch. "I know she's expecting me. I'm late."

"You's late?"

"Yes."

"Then good luck." He laughed. "You'll need it."

"Why?"

"She worshipped Lord Malcolm. He could do no wrong, and anyone who said otherwise got their knuckles rapped. Oh, and you'd better like cats."

"Cats?"

"Yes," said the man, and he narrowed his eyes. "You like cats?"

"Yes."

"Then you'll be all right." He ran his hands through his hair, pointed and said, "Go round the corner before the crossroads and follow your nose. You can't miss the place."

"Thank you."

"But mind you don't go anywhere but the house."

"I'm sorry?" I said.

"You would be if you do," he said, and then he turned his back on me, and went back to his work. I considered this riddle and wondered about the wisdom of asking another question, but I did not bother. I carried on down the road, around the church boundary towards my destination.

Belmont Hall stood at the end of its own drive, a large grey house with a castellated roof, ivy on the walls and tall mullioned windows. The drive skirted an orchard of apple trees, where a dozen ragged chickens scratched around their coop. Beyond this, a gate led into empty fields that climbed towards a wood. Standing and listening as I did, the sound was of sucking and bubbling, the ground trying in vain to soak up the pools of standing water that covered the land.

The front door was arched like a church door, with a polished knob and a heavy knocker made from the cast head of a lion. It was a knocker that dared you to use it, but I did not have to. Miss Watson had heard my approach and was waiting for me. A small woman with grey hair tied in a bun, she wore a chequered apron and had bright, darty eyes. She was a foot shorter than me, but had learnt the small person's trick of daring you to say what you were thinking and then nodding, because she knew exactly what you were thinking anyway. She nodded and was joined on the step by two cats, one black, one ginger. They were big and fit, and started sniffing my shoes before she yelled, "Slipper! Thomas! Come back!" and then said, "Mr Morris?"

"Yes."

"Good evening." Her lips were thin and her voice was clipped and clean. She spoke every word precisely, as if she was in constant danger of losing their meaning. "Welcome to Belmont." She took out a small pocket watch and squinted at it. "I was expecting you over an hour ago."

"I'm sorry. I got lost."

"Lost? The map was not clear enough?"

"No, the map was excellent. My driver abandoned me at Appley, and…"

"Your driver abandoned you?"

"Yes."

"But that's a disgrace. I've never heard anything like it. Did he explain why he did such a thing?"

"He wanted to return to Taunton before nightfall, and…" but before I had the chance to finish what I was going to say, she had disappeared inside and the cats had disappeared with her.

I followed and found myself standing next to a tall Chinese jar in a long, dark hallway. I know nothing about porcelain, but I know perfection when I see it, and this jar was old and perfect. It was covered in stylized or-ange birds and blue trees and small men carrying fishing rods. I almost touched it, but then I stopped myself and walked on.

The house was cool, and the smell of freshly baked cake hung in the air. I could hear running water and pots and pans being moved around. I followed the sounds and found Miss Watson in the kitchen. "I baked," she said, "and will put the kettle on in an hour." She gave me another of her glittery stares, wiped her hands on the corner of her apron, said, "Meanwhile, I'll show you to your room," and bustled past me, back down the hall and up the stairs to the landing.

She moved quickly. I followed. She left the smell of flour and violets in her wake. We walked down a long wood-panelled corridor, past closed doors and dark oil paint-ings to a room at the side of the house. "This is the guest room," she said. "I made the bed up and you can use the desk, but please" – she wagged a finger at me – "never open the windows."

"Why not?"

"It's a house rule. His Lordship never opened the windows. He didn't want moths eating his books."

"Moths?"

"Yes. He used to worry about them all the time."

"But moths don't eat books."

"The moths in these parts eat anything," she said, and her eyes shone, and then she turned and was gone, and I was left to stare out at the sodden fields and the sinking sun, and the chickens as they scratched and pecked through the muddied orchard below my window.

After I had drunk a cup of tea and eaten one of Miss Watson's cakes, I asked to see the library. She shook her head and told me I would have to wait until she had finished dusting. "Since his Lordship died," she said, "God rest his soul," and she crossed herself, "I've had to do everything. I don't think the family want anything to do with the place." I remembered the obituaries; he'd been widowed as a young man, and his only son had taken up with a bad lot. Now the new Lord Buff-Orpington was domiciled in London, by all accounts living a life of some debauchery. Sadness drifted into Miss Watson's eyes, coloured her face and twisted her lips into a bow. She pulled a handkerchief from her sleeve and dabbed her nose. I could not bear the thought of being so close to the library, but I knew arguing would be pointless, so I took a deep breath and said I would go for a stroll instead.

"Keep to the footpaths," she said.

"Of course."

"And close the gates behind you."

"Naturally."

"And whatever you do…" she said.

"Yes, Miss Watson?"

"Whatever you do, don't… don't go…" she said.

"Don't go where?" I said.

"There," she said, and she pointed outside, beyond the orchard and the chickens. "There. It's too... too..." but then she stopped herself and turned away, and her cats turned with her. Their tails were up and their fur was fine, and they knew exactly where to go. I opened my mouth as if to push her further, maybe even to insist she tell me what was on her mind, but it was too late. She and her cats had disappeared and I was left alone.

I strolled up the drive, opened and closed a gate and, ignoring her warning, walked through the orchard. The apple trees were loaded with ripening fruit and some of the chickens followed me. They clucked and bubbled, and then I was in the fields that sloped below the house.

The land was like a sponge, and I was forced to pick a crooked path towards the woods. Fat brown flies chased me, and the birds in the hedges were too tired to fly.

When I had walked half a mile, I turned to look back at Belmont. Its battlements shone and the bolted windows winked. The shelves of beautiful books waited for Miss Watson's duster, and they waited for me. I rolled up my sleeves and carried on down the path, over a fence and into the woods.

Maybe the old stories are true, the ones about hatted goblins stealing goats and children and hiding them in the cellars of damp houses in the woods. When I was a child my mother used to read fairy stories to me, and when she had tucked me in and blown the light out, I would lie in bed and worry myself to sleep. I would imagine the goblins lived in my wardrobe and would come out when I was not expecting them, and magic me to their black trees. And they would take me to secret dungeons in hidden hollows, tie me to a wall and threaten me with buckets of weasels. I was an only child and spent too much time frightened. The imaginary friends I created always turned out not to be friends at all, and would betray me to the worst characters in the stories I heard. So long ago – I thought – and then I thought it was no time at all. You carry the terror of childhood all your life, and nothing warns you that your mind is about to drop a bucket into its well. Old stories, big woods and dreams that fleece you.

Like the stories, the woods gave me a feeling of unease, as though I was being watched and my footsteps counted. The trees were tall and old, and away from the slippery path I could see patches of bramble. As I passed, birds stopped singing, mice stopped scurrying and the temperature dipped. The path dropped towards a stream in spate before climbing again, through trees that grew closer together. Their branches linked high above me and thick vines hung down, heavy with bearded seeds.

I tried to whistle, but my lips were too dry and the noise I made sounded like a slow puncture. The dipping sun splashed pools of light onto the ground, but these were overwhelmed by shadows. I reached a twitch on the path which seemed to be the place where I should turn and go back, but I could see the edge of the woods ahead, and a gate that led into a corn field.

So I carried on, under the last trees, through the gate and up to a narrow crest that gave me a view of the west. The course of the stream wound below me, and other patches of woodland filled the gaps between the fields and meadows.

At first sight, I did not see any sign of life, but as my eyes adjusted to the glare I saw the roof of a thatched house, partly hidden by the trees that surrounded it. The thatch was old and ragged, and its walls were unpainted. I sat down, and although I spent my time enjoying the view and wondering how long it would take to ride to the moors that cut the horizon, my eyes returned to the thatched house. Its windows were dark and a low wall surrounded a small garden. A ruined barn stood to one side and a gig stood in the drive. A cockerel crowed, and as I watched, one of the upstairs windows opened. The pane winked, a hand appeared, flicked a duster at the sky and then another hand closed the window. A dog barked a couple of times, then stopped, and for a moment the peace was absolute, as though spirits had come and taken a level of sense away. I do not know where the spirits went. Some hollow? Some cave? Some marsh where the water swallows itself and the sky comes down?

I waited for an answer but heard nothing, and waited for five more minutes before a bird called, another answered, and I turned around and walked back into the woods, under the trees and past the goblins' holes, over the stream until I reached the fields and the track to Belmont. The sun showed an edge of its disk through a cloud, then disappeared for good, and as the evening began to thicken towards the night, flies clouded around my head. And when I reached the house, the cats were standing by the front door with cruel looks in their eyes, and their tails up.

The library was dusted, the curtains drawn, candles lit and a long table had been cleared for me. An oak writing slope had been set up, and pens and paper arranged in a walnut tray. A beautiful silver ink well was filled. A leather-backed chair was by the table, and a studded wastepaper basket. The air smelt of lavender polish, and the peace of the room was only interrupted by the soft tick-tock of an old clock that stood on the mantelpiece.

The walls were lined with shelves and, where space allowed, dark paintings were hung. There were a pair of covetable seascapes – ships in distress, men clinging to rafts, waves lashing black cliffs – and some mountain views. A few portraits of severe men and women looked down at me, a fine copy of Largillière's *Voltaire as a Young Man* hung over the door, and a bust of the philosopher stood on a plinth by the window. He stared at me, his thin lips curled into a smile that dared me to put a price on his work. I looked back but said nothing to him. He was dead and buried, last words echoing, generous in his rot. Price or no price – I did not imagine he would have cared for polish.

Miss Watson was intimidated by the room, and the cats waited outside. They scowled at me, licked their lips and made low, growling noises. She spoke with a reverential voice. "His Lordship was not a religious man," she said, "but this was his church. He loved his books, loved them more than anything else in the world," and for a moment her eyes drifted away from mine. They fixed on some point on the other side of the room, and as she slipped into a sort of reverie, I pulled on my handling gloves, stepped to the nearest shelf, ran my fingers along the spines and stopped. The hair on the back of my neck froze. I was touching an edition of *Nouvelles probabilités en fait de justice*, published in Lausanne in 1772. I pulled it out, stroked its cover and held it to my nose. It smelt of cherries, and when I opened it at a random page, it gave a sigh, like it was waking from a long sleep and wanted to bathe, breakfast and enjoy conversation with an interesting person. A woman, maybe, someone who had lived in Geneva and Dublin, spoke five languages and had won and lost a few times. Swishing dresses, perfect hair, pink lips, rosy cheeks. Velvet and polished wood, wide linen sheets and the sound of water running into a bathtub. Steam rising, the promise of a glass of wine, candles, love, all these things. I sighed back at the book and said, "This is amazing. Incredible. As far as I know, there are less than a dozen copies of this edition. I had no idea. It's miraculous…"

Miss Watson went to the window, ran her fingers down the curtains and looked out. "Yes. His Lordship used to spend all day in here – towards the end he had me make up a bed in the corner." She pointed. "He couldn't bear to be away from his books."

I slid the book back onto the shelf, scanned the other volumes and said, "This is going to take me a while, longer than I thought."

Miss Watson inclined her head and said, "You must take as long as you need." She pulled a duster from her apron and flicked it at Voltaire's bust. Motes rose and fell, and the smell of furniture wax burst like a flower opening. "I must say, it is a pity you never met His Lordship. You two would have had such a lot to talk about. He knew so much about these books. He used to say there was more wisdom in this room than in any other room in the world; that made him happier than anything."

"Have you any pictures of him?"

"Oh yes," she said, "one or two," and she disappeared for a moment and came back with an envelope. She took out a photograph, stared at it for a moment and handed it to me. "This was made that last year. We visited the coast. It was such a lovely day."

Lord Malcolm was sitting on a bench. There was a gull in the sky above his head and he was staring at the sea. He had a small head, a splash of white hair emerging from his hat and a bright smile. He wore a smart coat, a scarf was wrapped around his neck, he was cradling a book in his arms, and although he looked relaxed there was an edginess to his appearance. Maybe he was there under duress, and all he wanted to do was go back to Ashbrittle and his library. But he had promised Miss Watson, and she would be disappointed if he cancelled the trip. She took the photograph back, touched the image with the tips of her fingers and said, "He was such a gentleman. So kind, so very distinguished," and a single tear formed in the corner of her right eye. "So distinguished..."

she said again. I opened my mouth to say something, but nothing came out, so she turned and left the room, and I was alone with the ticking, the polish and the dead man's books.

I worked for two hours. I say I worked, but this work was pure pleasure. When I discovered a copy of the rare first Irish printing of *Candide* (Dublin, 1759) I yelled with joy, and Miss Watson came running to see what the problem was, strands of hair escaping from her bun, wiping her hands on her apron.

I stroked the book and said, "A miracle is the violation of mathematical, divine, immutable, eternal laws. By this very statement, a miracle is a contradiction in terms."

"I beg your pardon?"

"Voltaire," I said. "And was he wrong?"

"Wrong?" she said, and she gave me a look that could have been pitiful. "I have no idea if he was right or wrong. I have other things to concern me."

I shook my head, rubbed the spine and the perfect tooling, but when I tried to explain she put up a hand and said, "I don't have to be told they're wonderful, but to me they are simply a great deal of dusting," and she shook her head and left me standing there with the book in my hand, the taste of a little triumph in my mouth and the long shadows of evening creeping across the garden.

I could have worked through the night, but after the Irish *Candide* I could not continue. My eyes hurt and my head was spinning. I felt a mix of tiredness and elation that creates harmonic echoes in my bones and brighter colours in the things I see. I put my notes away, took off my gloves, closed my eyes and listened to the house.

Candles fizzed, the windows twitched in their frames, and I heard the lazy pad of one of the cats as it crept down the corridor. The creak of a floorboard, a rustle of curtains, the squeak of a rusted hinge. All these noises came gently, swilled around and did not bother me. Although I loved my rooms in London, my life was dominated by noise. The rumble of traffic, the man downstairs playing his violin, another with a hacking cough. Stray dogs barking at the echoes of their own barking, angry men shouting at tearful women in the night. The indeterminate buzz in the city's air, bugs in the carpet and bubbles popping on the surface of a bar of soap – sometimes the city filled me with anger and frustration, and the attractions of the country were overwhelming, but I did not visit it enough. In those days I did not do anything enough. I did not listen hard enough and I did not look. I did not touch or feel and I did not love. I think I thought I had loved and could, but it is too easy to fool yourself into thinking one thing when you do the other. And then, without knowing, you realize everything you used to believe means nothing. It did not have to be a lie – it could have been the truth – but it was still as hollow or full as all the sounds of London, known or not, real or unreal, alive or dead.

My head was drowned in fatigue and Voltaire, and as I stood at the window to undress, the night slipped over the fields and the orchard below me and closed around the house. The moon was almost full and gave the land a milky, translucent glow. A few stars shone. I heard Miss Watson downstairs, talking to the cats. She scolded them like a mother would scold her children, instructed them to catch some mice and then closed the kitchen door and came upstairs. She walked slowly, and as she passed my room I heard her heavy breathing and the sound of her ankles clicking.

I blew out my candle, and as my eyes adjusted, the land shifted into sharper relief. I stretched my arms over my head, took a deep breath, closed my eyes, let the breath out and relaxed.

I listened to the air, stopped my thoughts, opened my eyes and focused. The land was still and quiet, steel-blue and grey. A cloud with the point of a knife drifted across the sky, and as it did a bird flapped out of a high tree. I watched it fly and turn and fall again, and it called out. Another bird replied and blew out of another tree. They circled for a moment and then started to climb into the sky, and as I watched them I felt myself drifting into the gap that lies between awake and dreams. Dreams of bats, days of books, dreams of wet boots lost in marshes, days of books. Sinking ships. Books. Father. School, terror. My legs were filled with wool and the palms of my hands were sweating. I blinked and rubbed my eyes, and when I looked again the birds were dots in the distance, far, far away.

I went to my bag, took out a bottle of whisky, poured a glass and went back to the window. I was going to open it but remembered Miss Watson's rule, so I rubbed the glass, downed the drink in one, said "sleep" to the window, turned and went to my bed. And after I had relaxed and the salt had drained from my mouth, I turned over, closed my eyes and drifted away to where the marshes and woods and books were illusions, and women rubbed their skin with honey.

My father used to call the parish church of St Michael, Dover, his office, and he was not an ironic man. In those days he did not know the meaning of the word. In those days he believed beauty was the work of the devil, grey was the colour of God, and coffee was drunk by heathens. With his enormous head, his booming voice, his dark suits and the ancient black horse that he rode until it collapsed and died under his feet outside Deal, he was, for a long time, a domineering and aggressive man. Many of his parishioners called him the Jeremiah of Kent and said his sermons offered inspiration, but I was scared of him and dreaded his "talks". These involved an invitation to his study, where I would be given a lecture on whatever subject was concerning him – the threat of dancing, the immorality of politicians, the danger of light operatics, the criminals who run banks – these are four examples of the subjects that vexed him, but there were more.

My mother was a delicate woman, dedicated to providing my father with the support he needed, but when I was ten, she was killed while doing some polishing. No one knows exactly how it happened, but she must have tripped and lost her balance, because she fell through a window, cut her arms and bled to death in a rose bed. I was at school when the accident happened, and came home to find the doctor talking to my father in the front parlour. When they looked at me their faces were grey, and I could tell. I was never one to miss the obvious. The warmth had left the house, and as he told me the news, father's eyes burned and his hair flared, and the doctor stared at the floor with his fingers turning white around the handle of his bag.

After the funeral, her picture disappeared from his bedside table, her dressing table and collection of floral plates were sold, and her clothes given away to the poor. His mouth pinched if I mentioned her, and I imagined his memories hid their eyes behind their hands. He did tell me that when I laid in bed and the night cracked at the window, I should remember she gave me my life and the best years of her life, and God wanted her to be with him. He wanted to read the list of her sins and praise the depth of her virtue. His mysterious plans are beyond our understanding, although we can believe they are always arranged with us in mind. For God is everything and we are simply his dust. He watches as we pour through his fingers, and smiles at our duality. He does not brood, and this is an important lesson, one we should never forget: do not brood, my son.

I did not think about brooding when I awoke. It was half-past seven and the light promised another damp, sucked day. Birds were singing, one hundred mad, bursting birds. I sat on the side of the bed and listened. I stood up, stretched, went to the window and opened the curtains. As I did, a gang of sparrows blew off the sill and disappeared over the roof. I put my hand on the latch and tried it. It moved a little. I looked over my shoulder, listened for Miss Watson and then carefully opened the window. It was stiff and squeaky, but when I had enough room I put my head out. Everything was as quiet as a quiet view of the country should be, like a picture on a wall or a plate in a book. I closed the window, dressed and went downstairs.

Miss Watson had cooked me a breakfast, and as I sat down to eat she said, "I trust you slept well?"

"I did, thank you."

She poured two cups of tea. "That would be Somerset air. Sweetest in the world."

I sliced a sausage, dipped it in the yolk of a fried egg and said, "Like a log." I put the sausage in my mouth and ate it.

Miss Watson turned away, went to the sink and began the washing up. She scrubbed a pan, rinsed it and dropped it on the draining board with a clatter. She picked up a plate and said, "Would you like more tea?"

"I'm fine."

"Fine?" she said, as if this was the first time she had heard the word.

"Yes."

She started to wash the plate and clicked her tongue against the roof of her mouth. She scrubbed the plate harder than she needed to, and when she had finished, put it on the draining board, turned towards me and wiped her hands on a dishcloth. I cut some bacon, laid it on a piece of fried bread and put it in my mouth. The fried bread was perfect.

"Well," she whispered, "if you say you are fine, then you must be," and she turned back to the sink, and with a sharp cough announced she was going into the village, and if I wanted anything I should give her a list.

"I have everything I need," I said.

"Well if you think of something…" she said, but I shook my head and turned to look at the cats. They were lying by the back door, and their cruel eyes stared at me as if they were planning murder, and all they needed was time and opportunity, and they did not care about fresh fish or any of the other foods people think they liked.

After breakfast I went to the library, stood at the window for a moment and looked out at the world. It was dull and cool, and a pale sun was failing to shine through the clouds. I turned, sat at the table, spread out my notes and closed my eyes. I watched the spots swarming in the dark, counted to twenty, opened my eyes and then went back to work.

Sometimes, I thought, it is impossible to tell the difference between the wishing and the well. Impossible? You know how it can be. You stare into the well and see yourself reflected in the water, and the water is deeper than you will ever be. Its surface is quiet and its depths are freezing, dark and lost. And what lies at the bottom of the well? A dead dog, a pile of tarnished coins, the rotted pages from a book no one reads any more. And the air between the surface and the brick edge of the well is filled with the echo of a silenced voice. I stopped thinking like this, and started to leaf through my notes. They whispered back at me. All those years, all those chapters, words, valuations, meanings. The house was still and quiet, and motes were dancing and chiming in their columns. I remembered the cakes my mother used to bake. Sponges steaming on the side, a bowl of icing waiting for a thieving finger. The gentle scrape of a chair on the kitchen tiles, sun reflected in a saucepan lid and the polished top of a kitchen table. Smells and memories, colliding in my head, turning me around and taking me away from my work.

The books waited and the books came, and within an hour I had discovered more remarkable treasures in Lord Malcolm's collection. The beauty of the set of *Œuvres* (Dresden, 1748), published under Voltaire's personal supervision, exceeded all my expectations. Each of the nine volumes had minor chips and scuffs, but their pages could have rolled off the presses yesterday, under his eye, under his thumbs. Some were foxed, but only lightly, and as I worked my way through them, it was easy to imagine supernatural elements at work, protecting and holding the books and their pages, the smudge of dead fingers and the scent of love.

The same thought occurred when I found a first of Rousseau's *Dissertation sur la musique moderne* (Paris, 1743). Once again, here was a book that could have been handled by its author, and as I turned the pages it was difficult to ignore the thought that my gloves were picking up traces of the man's skin. Maybe a flake from his forehead had dropped onto page 68 and been trapped in the gutter, and now its dust was released and drifting up my nose, down my throat and into my stomach. It sank into my gastric juices and joined the half-digested remains of breakfast. I noted the condition, likely reserve, and was about to slip it back on the shelf when I heard a single knock at the window.

I jumped. Miss Watson was staring in at me. She was carrying a basket and pointing up the drive. She was wearing a coat and a woollen hat, the strands of escaped hair were matted and sweat was pouring from her forehead. When I started to open the window she shook her head and shouted, "No!"

"I'm sorry..."

"I'll return after lunch," she said, "so help yourself to something from the larder," and without another word she was off, disappearing around the top of the drive, and then I was alone in the house, and the cats could have been mine.

I thought about the cats but left them alone. They meant nothing to me, with their hairballs and eyes and the way they padded around and waited for nothing in particular. I worked hard, and after lunch – some hunks of bread and cheese and a glass of lime cordial – I walked into Ashbrittle.

I stood in front of the house and scanned the orchard, the field beyond, and followed the line of the sodden path into the woods. Leaves rustled in the lightest breeze, a rabbit hopped along the line of a hedge, stopped, stared and disappeared into a thicket. A bird called, but only once. I walked up the drive, into the lane, past the outlying houses, round the bend, around another and into the village.

The air was sour, as though it had been borrowed from a forgotten larder, and the hedges were full of a damp must. This drifted in small, private clouds and settled on the leaves and twigs. I sneezed once.

I strolled past a line of cottages into the churchyard and visited the famous yew tree with its healing powers and branches spreading over the graves.

It grew from a small burial mound. I climbed up, ducked down and stood inside the forks made from the cracked trunk. The bark was flaked and pale and running with ants. Once, the warm guts of living men were nailed here and the men forced to walk around the tree, unravelling their entrails, bees humming, women laughing and yelling to their mad gods, children in lines singing pretty songs. Gods looking on, laughing back and nodding satisfaction and waiting for the next man to be brought for slaughter. The blood running, dogs howling and waiting to eat, sweet smells in the air. Music played on instruments people smashed and burned a long time ago. Purple. I believe the world was purple in those days, but now the colour was green and it was cool in there like a still draught, and birds chirped in the branches. Someone had put a posy in a crack in the bark, little yellow and blue flowers that had faded now. I touched them, petals dropped away and the church clock began to chime the hour.

One.

Two...

Two chimes. They echoed across the valley below and, as I listened I saw an old woman come from her house, scatter corn for her hens and look towards me. She was wearing a woollen hat on her head and a long ragged coat. She watched me for a minute and took off her hat. Her hair spilt out like water from a jug, down her back to her waist. She smiled at me, but I knew she did not want to know me. She smiled as though she knew something I did not but would not breathe a word, not a single word. Her eyes were cold and hard, and her face lined. I thought I was looking at the face of a witch and supposed she read my mind. She took her hair in one hand, twisted it into a knot, tucked it up and put her hat on. Then, as I turned away from her, she went back inside and slammed the door. A dog barked at a cat. The sun was wet. The bells faded. The day faded too.

After my mother's death, my father's behaviour became increasingly strange and irrational; one day he announced to his congregation that church bells were un-Christian and, rather than serve as a call to worship, tempted people to turn away from God. Their noise was an anathema to the Almighty and distracted from sincere prayer, so the next day he disconnected the mechanism that controlled the chimes, hid it in a cupboard and refused to entertain campanologists. This caused an outcry in Dover, and petitions were written to the Bishop, who wrote to inform my father that he had no authority to incapacitate the bells and was to restore them to working order immediately.

The Bishop was a thin man who arrived at the vicarage in a fine black carriage with purple curtains, but father locked the front door and refused to speak to him or accept his authority in the matter. For over eight years, the issue of St Michael's bells vexed Kent's ecclesiastical authorities, until the problem of declining congregations became a more pressing issue and my father's behaviour was consigned to the back of the stove.

I thought about my father simmering while I listened to Ashbrittle's bells, and when they had finished chiming and their echoes had disappeared over the graves, I climbed down from the yew mound, crossed the lines between a memory I had, another I imagined and all the others pouring out of the ground, and walked through the graveyard to a gate that led into the fields.

I was going to return to my work but did not. I was pulled on. My feet had their own ideas and my eyes wanted to follow. I climbed over the gate, crossed the fields and found myself on the path that led to the woods. When I reached the first trees, I stopped and turned to look back at Belmont. The library windows blinked at me, the books were silent in their rows. Spines and pages and marbling. The scent of wax, the dark oak panelling, the leather-backed chairs. The pictures on the walls, the carpets on the floors, the light dust of flour drifting in the kitchen. The cats snoozed on the garden wall and waited for Miss Watson's return. They sneered, and I sneered, hissed and turned my back.

The woods were damp and still, and when I reached the tumbling river, I followed it for a while and found some curious pebbles on the muddy bank. They were lying in little groups like families of stone, round, transparent and covered in speckles. Some of them were pitted and others were perfectly smooth. I picked one up and rolled it in the palm of my hand, put it in my pocket and carried on until I came to a place where a spring was bubbling from the ground. Lush plants were growing all around, their leaves dipping in the water and bobbing in a light draught that blew up the path. I stopped to scoop some water, splash my face and drink. It was sweet and cool. Then I climbed up through a hall of hanging vines and brambles towards the top of the wood.

When I reached the crest, I sat to watch the west and the thatched house below me. Its chimney was still smoking, the windows were still dark and closed, and as I watched I saw a man walking towards me. He was carrying a walking stick, swishing at nettles, hurrying through the field, his eyes fixed on me all the way. For a moment I considered ducking back into the woods and walking back the way I had come. I was not in the mood for conversation, and all I wanted to do was sit down and watch the land and the sky, but when he got close enough I suddenly called "Good afternoon!" as though I had no choice.

When he reached me, he looked me up and down, paused, ran his hands through his hair and took deep, panting breaths. For some reason, no particular reason, I expected him to walk on without saying anything – a wild, odd man with better things to do than talk – but then he smiled and said, "And a good afternoon to you."

I held out my hand, he wiped his on his trousers, we shook, and he said, "Professor Hunt. Professor Richard Hunt." His hand was ice-cold, his skin was too smooth for a man of his age and his face had a sucked-in, skeletal look. His hair was dark and thin and combed carefully over the crown of his balding head. I guessed he must have been sixty, but he could have been forty-five.

"David Morris," I said.

"David Morris…" he said, as if he was trying to remember my name from somewhere else, some other field or town or a dignified occasion where men in evening dress and women in beautiful frocks had drunk exotic drinks and talked about nothing in particular.

"Yes."

"And you're on your holiday?" He was dressed in a brown woollen suit, a check shirt and a red tie, and spoke with a polished, even voice. I assumed he was English, but an edge to his accent made me think he was German, maybe, or Austrian. His eyes were grey and cunning and looked straight into mine. There was something guarded about his manner, but he was working hard to be open and friendly.

"No," I said. "I'm working at Belmont."

"Ah, Belmont."

"Yes."

"Such a superb house. It must be one of the most beautiful in the county. And such a wonderful atmosphere, don't you think? A calm, civilized air about the place."

"Yes," I said.

He smiled at me. "And what are you doing there?"

"I'm cataloguing Lord Malcolm's library."

"That must be such interesting work. He had so many wonderful books. We didn't know each other for very long, but I think I can say Lord Malcolm was a good friend of mine. I do miss our conversations. He was such a gentleman."

"That's what I've heard."

"I don't think he had a bad word to say about anyone – or anything, for that matter."

"I never met him," I said, "but I wish I had."

"Mmm," said Hunt, and he smiled again. "I'm sure you do. He was a man who understood what it is to be great." Hunt put emphasis on this last word and puffed out his chest. "You must understand, greatness is inborn, it can never be given. Some people even say it can be bought, but no. Never."

"I think…" I started, but Hunt interrupted.

"I've been saying this for a long time, and some people said I didn't know what I was talking about. Me?" He held his stomach and laughed at the idea. "I wouldn't think so." He stopped laughing as quickly as he had started.

"And now you live here?"

"Yes," he said, and he pointed towards the house below. "And that is where I am going now. I like a walk after lunch, but must get back to work now."

"What do you do?"

"Do?"

"Yes."

"I do not do, young man. I work. I create."

"My apologies. What do you create, Professor Hunt?"

He took a step towards me, lowered his voice and said, "I would not tell you, even if I could. But suffice to say it is a marvel." I thought he was going to continue, but he stopped suddenly, looked straight into my eyes and shook his head.

"I see," I said.

"No," he said, "you do not. How could you?"

"I..."

"How could you even begin to see?"

"I didn't mean to imply..."

"I am sure you didn't."

"...that I know..."

"Of course you didn't," he said and he turned, bowed politely, took a couple of steps back, and before I had the chance to ask him anything else, he signalled the end of the meeting with a raised hand and said "It was very interesting to meet you. It's good to talk to someone with something to say. Too many of the people round here are idiots. Idiots and fools. You cannot talk to any of them..." And then he was gone and I was left standing alone. I opened my mouth and was about to tell him that I had not said anything interesting, but he disappeared, and when I saw him next he was far below me, walking across the fields towards his house.

I turned and was heading back to Belmont when I saw something twinkling on the ground. I stooped to pick it up. It was a gold tiepin, set with a single diamond. There was a Latin inscription on the back. I read the words: *Væ puto deus fio*. I cupped my hands over my mouth to shout, but Hunt had disappeared again, so I put the pin in my pocket and walked back into the woods, with the leaves as green as black, and the fevered streams and springs.

I worked for a few hours. I had catalogued the most important books in the collection and was working on the first shelf of lesser volumes when Miss Watson came back from the village. She stood by the kitchen table and refused to let me make her a cup of tea. She said it was her job and always had been, and she was not changing the way she worked simply because Lord Malcolm had died. I had no choice but to sit and wait until she had stored the shopping away, and then she put the kettle on the stove.

As we drank our tea and ate cake, I asked Miss Watson about Professor Hunt. She spluttered and slammed the table with her hand. "Was he here?"

"No."

"Because he's not welcome."

"I met him in the woods…" I began, but she interrupted.

"He's not to be trusted."

"He seemed pleasant enough."

"But of course he did. His Lordship thought he was pleasant enough too, but that didn't stop him from taking advantage."

"How?"

Miss Watson stared out of the kitchen window, looked down at the cats and shook her head. "It's a long story," she said, "but I've no time now." She slapped her knees and stood up. The cats opened their eyes, looked at her, blinked at me and shut them again. "No time. And you… shouldn't you be working?"

"Yes," I said, "I suppose I should be."

"Then go. Go back to your work."

My father used to tell me to work hard, play games and pass exams, and when I was thirteen I won a scholarship to a minor public school in Dorset. As the only child of a widowed parson, I was the half-dreamer who sat near the back of the class, stared out of the window at the hills and trees, only spoke when spoken to, and absorbed lessons without thinking.

It was during this period of my life that I discovered my passion for books. The school had a good library, and I worked my way through the shelves like a ferret. I read anything – and by my sixteenth birthday had wandered from the obscure to the popular, the dangerous to the anodyne, stopping at all the major stations on the way.

My love of books did lead me into trouble, but when I returned to Dover for the holidays, and my father ceremoniously opened and read my masters' report, he seemed disappointed that none had a bad word to say about me. Maybe I am being hard on him, and maybe he always had my best interests at heart. And maybe he was frustrated, working all his life in Dover, without the chance to move to a comfortable parish in the West Country where the yews spread, the dogs wink and he could visit his parishioners on a sleek black mare. But at the time I did not know what frustration was, and I thought I was a nuisance to him and he had hardened his heart against me. I did not know he had only removed my mother's picture to a locked drawer and took it out and stared at it when he was alone, and touched the image of her face with his fingers. And that one day he would find salvation in archery.

Holidays. I remember the salt air stinging my face in August, and the smell of the housekeeper's honest cooking. She was called Miss Pringle and would arrive in the afternoon to clean the house, do the laundry and cook the evening meal. A quiet and pious woman, I think I only heard her say half a dozen words, and then in a whisper. She hummed softly as she worked, mainly hymns, but occasionally tunes I did not recognize. She did not have children of her own, and was always very kind to me. I think she might have been a disgraced nun, or someone who was waiting for someone else she used to love, maybe still loved. Sometimes she brought sugar lumps to work with her and offered one to me when father's back was turned. He believed sugar was another of the Devil's instruments, and should be avoided at all costs. He would say, "It's not just your teeth that will rot," but would not elaborate. He did not like to elaborate: if the message was unclear, then this was the listener's fault.

I worked through the afternoon, and now and again I took Hunt's tiepin out of my pocket and turned it over in my hand. It was a curious thing, made from a curl of delicately worked old gold, with the diamond set at the widest end.

I recognized the inscription on the back – *Væ puto deus fio* – from school. "*Oh, I think I'm becoming a God.*" These were Vespasian's last words, spoken from a wide bed in a cool room overlooking the dewy fields of the Sabine country. With his suppurating legs and the boils on his face, the old Emperor died in pain but wonder, and as he gasped his final breath he doubted the wisdom of his priests. One of my classics masters used to return to the good pagan again and again, citing him as one of Rome's greatest reformers. From the military to the law courts, the man had taken the tottering empire and put it back on its feet. He made his name as a brutal oppressor of the Jews, but his later tolerance of the religion paved the way for Christianity's growth. Indeed, Vespasian's granddaughter, Flavia Domitilla, is still revered by the Catholic church as saint and her lonely banishment on a Tyrrhenian island is held up as an early example of Christian fortitude and constancy.

Sometimes my work as a book valuer was like a bag over my head, blinding and suffocating me with an endless parade of half-remembered truths, stories and lies. As the evening failed and the night crept over the hills and touched the windows, I put the tiepin in my pocket and left Belmont for Professor Hunt's house. I told Miss Watson I would be back for supper, but did not tell her where I was going. She said she was serving cold cuts and cheese, so I did not have to worry about anything spoiling.

The light shifted from milky- to steel-blue, and birds chattered before settling down for the night. Between the shifting, loaded clouds, the moon appeared. It was creeping towards full, like a bucket holding water, tipping towards me and the path, pouring its light down.

As I headed across the fields to the woods, I heard a scurrying and watched a pair of rabbits scamper ahead of me, but when I reached the trees, a half-silence came down like a blanket, and all I could hear was the sound of the burbling stream, my shoes squelching in the ground, and my breathing.

I felt uneasy as I walked, but did not feel I was watched or my steps were counted, and when I reached the crest of the hill, I did not stop. Candles were burning in Hunt's house, the chimney was smoking, and as I headed down the other side of the hill I heard a piano. Someone was playing Bach, a transcription from St Matthew's Passion. I stopped to listen and was reminded of home, for when I lived with my father, he hummed the oratorio endlessly. He disliked many types of music – he thought opera could sap the will to live and that music-hall performers were more dangerous than Catholics – but he loved Bach. He believed the man's harmonic explorations proved – if proof was required by the faithless – the existence of God.

"Bach recognized his gift as divine," he would say, "so if we listen closely, we can hear Christ's voice in his."

Before Father took this theory any further, I would go for a walk if I could.

Bach was a great walker. With his wig thrown back and his breeches flapping, he found consolation in long walks.

A digression. Towards the end of my time as a book valuer, I was asked to travel to Germany. It was a long trip, but the music department was short-staffed, so I was given a background briefing to the history of German music and sent to the town of Arnstadt to look at some manuscript scores that had surfaced in the collection of a dead organist. Many were based on work by Goethe, and included an autograph sketch from Wagner's *Faust Overture*. I also found manuscripts by Liszt, Mendelssohn, Spohr and Zelter, and when

I had completed an outline valuation I visited the church where Bach had worked as organist. A guide explained that the man had had a light schedule in Arnstadt, and one day had set out to walk 250 miles to visit a colleague in Lübeck. The journey took him ten days, and when it was time for him to return, he stayed for an extra three months.

I remember lying on my hotel bed, nursing my mouth, thinking about Bach's feet soaking in a bowl of warm salt water. Earlier in the day, I had been stung on the tongue by a wasp that had found its way onto my plate of veal and cabbage, and although I was no longer in pain I was still feeling sorry for myself, so far from home and alone on a strange bed in a dim room with faded prints on the wall.

Hunt's garden was more overgrown than it looked from a distance, and the gate was stuck. I had to lift it off its hinges to get in, then put it back and stumbled through a mass of weeds and grasses, rambling roses and honeysuckle to the front step. There was no knocker, so I banged on the door with my fist and took a step back.

I waited for a moment. There was no answer, so I knocked again. The Bach stopped suddenly, like the man himself had simply fallen down a hole in the middle of the road, wig off, breeches ripped. There was movement inside the house. I heard what sounded like a piece of wood being scraped across gravel and then it stopped, and a moment later a bolt was drawn back, keys jangled, a lock turned and the door opened a crack. A voice said, "Yes?"

"Professor Hunt?"

"Who is this?"

"David. David Morris. We met this afternoon. I'm working at Belmont."

"Ah, Mr Morris. The cataloguer. How are you today?"

"I'm well."

"Excellent," he said, and he opened the door wide. As he did, a strange, thick smell drifted out. At first I thought it was burning almonds, then I thought it was roses and then I could not decide what it was. It was sweet and stale, clung to the inside of my nostrils and would not let go. My eyes began to run, and then I was hit by a blast of heat – mad, boiling heat. I took a step back and, as I did, my eyes adjusted to the hallway that stretched out in front of me. There were no pictures on its walls or carpets on the floor, and I was overwhelmed by the feeling that this house was unloved and unholy. Hunt was wearing a white coat and wiping his hands on a towel. "I apologize," he said. "I would ask you in, but I'm in the middle of something and…"

"No," I said, "I didn't mean to interrupt you, but…" The smell suddenly caught in my throat. I stopped talking and gagged.

"But?"

"But," I said, "I found this, and, well, assumed it was yours." I took the tiepin out of my pocket and placed it in the palm of my hand. "I think you may have dropped it." It winked at me, once.

His eyes changed quickly when he saw the pin, and he smiled as he reached out and took it from me. He turned it over and squinted at the inscription, then polished it on his sleeve. "Oh, thank you," he said. "Thank you so much. I was going quite mad with worry. I tried to remember where I had been, who I had seen, but you know how it is. It's so easy to forget, and this is so precious to me."

"I thought it would be," I said.

"It is."

"Well..."

"It was presented by my colleagues when I left Cambridge." His eyes swivelled away from me and then, suddenly, I sensed he was telling a lie.

"You worked in Cambridge?"

"Yes," said Hunt. "You know the place?"

"I've visited."

"Quite the most beautiful city in the country," he said.

"Yes, it is lovely," I said, but I was not really thinking about it. Sweat was pouring down my back, and now all I wanted to do was to get back into the fields and woods. The smell of almonds or roses was growing more powerful, and I did not wait to be offered anything, so I turned and stepped back. I took one step, then another, and as I took a third I heard a whimper, a long, low wheeze of pain that started quietly and then disappeared.

At first I thought it came from a cat or a dog, an animal locked in a cupboard, and while I waited to hear claws scratching down the back of a door, I heard a pair of quick, short gasps and then a woman's scream, a scream of such pain that every hair on my body stood on end and the blood flushed from my face. She was upstairs, directly above me. I heard the scrape of her feet and the bang of her head or something against the wall. The scream reached a pitch that threatened to shatter the windows, and then it faded back to the whimper. "Good Lord!" I said. "Who's that?"

"Who's what?"

"That!" I said. "Who's screaming?"

"Oh," he shook his head, lowered his voice and took a step towards me, "that... that is my sister."

"Your sister?"

"Yes. I'm afraid so."

"Is she... she..."

"She's unwell."

"She sounds in pain."

"That's because she is," he said.

The whimper came again.

"What's... what's her illness?"

He shook his head, and a grim cloud drifted into his eyes. "She recently returned from India. She contracted malaria in Calcutta, and it has fallen upon me to nurse her – hopefully – back to health."

"Hopefully?"

"She has been close to death."

"Oh," I said. "I'm sorry."

"So am I. She is so dear to me." He held up the pin, said "Thank you so much for this" and started to close the door.

"If I can be of any assistance," I said.

He held the door half open. "That's kind of you, but I think I have all I need. However, if I do need to call on you, maybe I could leave word with Miss Watson."

"Of course."

"But for now I must ask you to let me get back to her," and with that, he closed the door, and I was alone in the garden again.

I started to walk, but was no farther than the gate before I heard the scream again, fainter now but just as desperate and sad. I turned and stopped, and scanned the upstairs windows.

Light was escaping through the cracks in one of the curtained windows, and I saw a shadow move against it. It stopped, it stayed and then it was gone and the light was gone. I went through the gate and into the fields and found myself half-running in a panic, up the hill and into the woods, under the trees and splashing through the stream and down the other side, and I could hear my mother's calm voice in my head, telling stories about branches that grab and cling, houses of sugar and goblins waiting with copper pots, and I heard her voice ringing in my head until I could see Belmont's lights shining at me. Miss Watson's cats were at the back door, crying around my feet as I stumbled into the house, clattered through the kitchen and climbed the stairs to my room.

I had a bad, frightening night. I lay awake for an hour and wondered: was Hunt too convincing? A convincing nurse or a convincing liar? Could a malarial woman sit up, let alone have the strength to scream? And what was that smell? And who made the ghostly shadow against the half-lit curtains? And as my questions and thoughts swept one way and the other, the lonely scream echoed in my head. It would not leave me, and as it grew, I stared at the moon as she failed through the dark. Her colours twisted and swirled from cream to blue and milk and white, and when clouds crossed her face she winced. She winced and maybe I heard her sigh. I do not know, but when I fell asleep, my dreams were filled with darker sighs and screams, and the music of a deep, endless loss. A woman was there, locked in a cage. She was holding the bars, looking at me, mouthing words and making signs with her hands. Dogs were there too, chained to walls, snarling and rearing on their back legs. They were barking at me, and as I tried to work my way around them, Hunt appeared and started shouting at me. He yelled about respect and intelligence and how people like me were worms, and when I looked at the ground it was crawling with maggots. They were making a low, slithering noise, and some of them started to climb my legs. I tried to brush them off, but they would not go away, and the more I brushed the more they climbed. I opened my mouth to yell, but my voice stuck and nothing came out. The dogs did not stop barking, the woman did not stop mouthing and moving her hands. I tried to take a step towards her, but I was stuck, the worms were climbing higher, I felt one work its way inside my collar and climb down my spine. I opened my mouth again and as I did I started awake.

Sweat was pouring down my face, the heat was overwhelming and my body was paralysed. My sheets, blankets and pillows were scattered across the floor. I tried to move, but could not. My arms and legs felt as though they were bolted to the bed, and my eyes were frozen open. I stared at the ceiling and tried to speak, but my tongue would not move and my lips were broken. This state lasted for another hour, and then I was asleep again and in a different dream. The same woman was there, but now she had a voice and she was wailing at me, pleading and waiting. "Help!" she called. "Please, help me…" I listened, but there was nothing I could do.

When the morning came, I joined Miss Watson for breakfast, but I was exhausted and could not eat. She was angry and said "What time did you get in?" with a snap to her voice that made me sit up and wince.

"I'm sorry," I said, "but I've no idea."

"It was late."

"I know. I had a…"

"A what?"

"A…" I said, but I could not explain. The words stuck in my throat like little bones.

She wagged a finger and said, "His Lordship was an extremely hospitable gentleman, but he would not have approved. Stumbling back in the middle of the night, crashing and banging on the stairs. I never heard anything like it. The cats were beside themselves, and as for me... I don't like to say what I thought. Burglars, anyone..."

"It won't happen again," I said.

She sipped some tea. "I should hope not."

"But I was out."

"So you were saying..."

"I went to visit Professor Hunt and had a very strange..."

"Excuse me?"

"I saw Professor Hunt again. I found his tiepin."

"You found his tiepin?"

"Yes. He dropped it yesterday. I was returning it."

Miss Watson stood up from the table and went to the cooker. She said, "I knew you were up to no good. I knew it. I should have told you."

"Told me what?"

"Not to go over there."

"And why would you have told me that?"

"Because... because he is not to be trusted," she said, and she slammed a frying pan on the stove and crossed her arms. "Not after what he did."

"And what was that?" Now I raised my voice. "Last night, while I was over there, I heard someone screaming. A woman. Upstairs in the house. She sounded in pain."

"A woman?"

"Yes. He said she was his sister. And he said she was malarial, suffering..."

"Malarial? What is that?"

69

"Malaria is a tropical disease. He said she caught it in India."

She huffed and said, "I've no idea about India and no idea what goes on over there, no idea at all. Maybe the Professor has a sister, maybe not. But I do know His Lordship leant him some books, and that was something he never did. He would have sooner leant money than one of his books; God knows how Hunt persuaded him. And that was the last His Lordship ever saw of them. Of course, he was too much of a gentleman to ask for their return. I believe he wrote letters, but they did no good. No good at all. Hunt!" Miss Watson spat the name. "It wouldn't surprise me if he did have a sick sister over there. Nothing would surprise me about him. Nothing..." And when I opened my mouth to ask another question she shook her head before I could speak, and I was left to blink at the day, and I wished the floor would open up and a bed would appear and I could be laid down by gentle hands. I did think this, but the floor remained solid, so I left the kitchen and Miss Watson, and went to the library.

I worked for an hour but could not concentrate. The books blurred and the birds sang outside the window. The latch was padlocked. Once or twice I left the library, went outside and stood in the drive. I considered my choices. If I ordered a gig, I could be at Taunton station in time for the last train, and home before nightfall. Ah, home. Comfort, peace. I was thinking about the pleasures of familiarity when I heard the sound of an approaching carriage. I stood and watched as it came into view, turned and stopped in front of the house. The driver climbed down and opened the door for a top-hatted man in an immaculate black suit. I took him for an undertaker, but he introduced himself as Mr Prior-Stewart, the lawyer charged with the business of Lord Malcolm's probate. As we were shaking hands, Miss Watson appeared at the front door. She made a pretence of ignoring me, and as she showed the gentleman in, I caught his eye and he pursed his lips and gave me the faintest of smiles, as if he understood me very well and I was not to feel slighted. Slighted? I did not feel slighted, but I was left with the thought that I did not wish to return to my work.

I walked to Ashbrittle, sat in the graveyard and listened to the sound of the wind rustling through the yew. I saw the red-haired man I had seen before, but he did not stop to talk. He was digging and whistling as he worked, and two birds were sitting on the wall behind him, waiting for the likely worm or beetle, flying away and then back again, and calling between themselves. There was a vague, hazy feeling in the damp air, warm but with a cold edge, like red turning to white. Or something. I could not put my finger on it, but I tried to. I tried very hard, like a child tries to thread a needle, or a dog tries to catch a cat in a tree. Although I was there I felt parted from the scene, as if I was looking at a picture, not a reality. Or, again, something.

I had planned to go back to Belmont, but I changed my mind again, went through the village and down the hill, and the sky and hedges led me on. I reached a bridge over a river. I stood and watched the water, listened to the breeze in the trees and thought about London. I had a day's work left to do and then I could return without worrying about whether I had abandoned the work. I looked at my watch. It was half-past twelve, so I carried on walking, past a straggle of poor, ruined houses to the crossroads at Appley. I was trying to decide whether I should chance a drink at the public house or turn round and return to Ashbrittle, when I heard a carriage. I stood on the verge to let it pass. The driver slowed, the window opened and Mr Prior-Stewart put his head out and said, "Can I offer you a lift?"

"Thank you," I said, "but no. I was just taking the air."

"Are you quite sure? I was considering some refreshment. Apparently Mrs Beck draws a fine cider."

"Mrs Beck?"

"At Appley."

"Well," I said, "I am tempted. Lord Malcolm's library does induce a fair thirst."

"Then climb in," he said.

Mrs Beck and her dog remembered me, and as I waited for our drinks, she asked if Miss Watson had packed her bags. When I asked why Miss Watson would have packed, I was

told that now the new Lord Buff-Orpington was moving to
Belmont, the place would be changing and she would no
longer be needed. The house would be transformed, the old
times and ways would be swept away, and nothing would be
the same again. The orchard would be lawned, and tennis
courts would be built. Mr Prior-Stewart smiled and shook
his head but did not say anything, and the other customers
– two florid labourers – looked us up and down and wiped
their mouths with the backs of their hands. We took our
drinks outside and sat at a table in a shaded corner of the
garden, and I said, "Tennis courts?"

"Who knows?" said Mr Prior-Stewart. "She's been listening to gossip. But whatever happens, Lord Henry will want
to keep Miss Watson on. That's what I came to tell her."

"She'll be relieved."

"She is."

"Good. I've no idea what she would do if she was forced
to leave Belmont. It's been her life."

"She's a treasure."

"Yes," I said, and we raised our glasses to her.

The cider was sour and foxed with thin strands of a
jelly-like substance – a good sign, my companion explained
– but I was inclined to take small sips and merely pretend
to enjoy the stuff as we talked. I spoke about my work,
the library and the masters of the French Enlightenment,
and he told me about his work and how he had moved
to Taunton when he had qualified, but was fast coming
to the conclusion that the town was too small for him.

The people – he explained – were stifling him, and his rooms were far too small. The attractions of the country had waned, and he supposed he was a city person. "Always was, always have to be…" he said, and I wanted to listen, but as he talked, my mind started to wander back to the events of the night, and I heard the scream in my head again.

"…so I am planning my return to London. I thought I could settle here, but I was mistaken. Wandering from one boring case to the next. A move seems the sensible thing."

"I see."

"And then I shall be able to…"

"Last night," I blurted, "I had a very strange experience. It was quite frightening, quite disorientating."

"Excuse me?"

"No," I stuttered. "Forgive me. You were talking about moving." I sipped the cider and winced. "Back to London?"

"What happened?" Mr Prior-Stewart moved towards me and gave me a look of concern. "Where were you?"

"In the fields behind Belmont. I met someone. A professor. At least, so he claims."

"His name?"

"Professor Hunt."

"Of course," he said.

"You know him?"

He narrowed his eyes and nodded his head. "Oh yes. We represented him."

"Why?"

"Because," he said.

"Have you met him?"

"Once. He came to the office."

"What do you know about him? Miss Watson won't tell me anything."

"Nor can I," he said, and he gave me a line about the oath of confidentiality he had been obliged to take before entering his profession, but it faded away as he spoke it. He looked one way and then the other, lowered his voice and said, "He's a Professor of the Sciences. He moved here from Cambridge. He was working at the university, but from what I heard, you know..."

"No I don't," I said.

"He left under a cloud."

"Did he?"

"Apparently."

"Any idea what sort of cloud?"

He shrugged and ran his fingers through his hair. It broke across his forehead and spilt into his eyes. "I have no idea. Why? Did he have something to do with your strange experience?"

"Yes," I said, and I told him about the sodden woods, the tiepin, the house, the scented heat and the scream. I told him about running back through the woods, but most of all I talked about the scream, the way it had cut through the night and its lonely pitch. And I said I had dreamt the worst dreams and now the cider was going to my head, and all I wanted to do was spend the rest of the afternoon lying in a dark room. But I had work to do. I had to get back to Belmont and I had been wasting his time, but he did not agree and said, "I understand he's in dispute with the farmer who owns the fields behind his house. He believes he has rights of access."

"Has he?"

He shrugged.

"Do you know anything about a sister?"

"No."

"Apparently she's staying with him, and he claimed she's malarial, but I don't know. I felt he wasn't telling me everything. I believe malaria induces tiredness, and I don't know, but…"

"But what?"

"I had the strangest feeling."

"Of what?"

"Of deception."

"And what made you think that?"

"Something in his manner." I stared into my cider, swirled it and said, "I thought, whoever she is, whether his sister or not, she certainly doesn't want to be there."

"You are sure you heard a woman scream? Not a bird?"

I shook my head and said, "Do I look like I'd mistake a bird for a woman? Please, Mr Prior-Stewart. I know what a screaming woman sounds like."

"And you've heard a few, have you?"

"You," I said and I pointed at him, "know what I mean." I did not mean to point. It was a rude thing to do, something my father would have chided me for. But I had made the mistake and now it was too late.

"I," he said, pointing back, "have no idea what you mean. I met you for the first time this morning, and now you're expecting me to read your mind."

"No I'm not," I said, thinking that under different circumstances he and I could have been friends, but now my boats were burning in their harbour. The flames were leaping into the air and it was too hot to stand on the quay. Fish were leaping and sad ballads were being sung by men in long dark coats. Candles blew out but there was no breeze. No breeze at all. Women turned their backs and climbed long streets to tiny houses. Empty rigging flamed, creaked, snapped and dropped into the water. Low birds were caught in the flames and fell out of the sky. The fire was reflected on the water, which was perfectly calm. "I'm not at all. I heard a woman screaming in Hunt's house."

"So what are you going to do?"

"I've no idea," I said and I drank some more cider. "No idea at all." And it was true. I had lived a quiet life and was not used to this type of excitement. "No idea at all," and as our conversation petered into silence, I took out my watch, checked the time and said, "I should be returning to my work."

"Already?"

"Yes," I said, and stood up.

"I suppose," he said, "you could always ask Miss Watson about the Professor. I understand he and she had some, how can I put this, agreement..."

"What do you mean?"

"Exactly what I say."

"She seems to have nothing but contempt for the man."

"It didn't use to be that way."

"How did it use to be?"

"Well, I hesitate to speculate…"

"Or gossip?"

"I never gossip, sir, never. As a solicitor, it would be impossible for me."

I almost laughed.

"No," he said. "Lord Malcolm told me the story before he died, and he was unimpeachable."

"So?"

So, shortly after Professor Hunt moved to the area, he called on Lord Malcolm to pay his respects. The two men found each other's company agreeable, and when Miss Watson was introduced, she was particularly interested in the newcomer, as her father had once lived in Cambridge. They talked about the city, the colleges, the river and the Backs – and when, a week later, Hunt called again, he asked her if she would be able to do some food-shopping for him. Although she said she was already quite busy enough, she agreed: "As long as I don't have to carry sacks of potatoes."

"I don't eat starch," said the Professor. "Potatoes. I don't eat potatoes."

So Miss Watson started to do his shopping, cycling with his basket and carrying it back to Belmont on her bicycle.

He was insistent that she did not have to deliver to his house. "I can't have you walking through the fields," he said, "if I could collect it from your kitchen, that would be splendid," and she decided this considerate and intelligent man had some – if not all – of the qualities she liked in a man. In her mind it would have been indecent to think about men, but something about Hunt drew her in and would not let go. Was it his precise, deliberate way of talking, or his shrewd, intelligent eyes? Or the quality of his suits? The polish of his brogues? She didn't know, and the more she thought about him, the more confused she became. She was unsure of her feelings, surprised by them, so one day she resolved to carry his shopping to his house. She was curious to know how he lived, what sort of furniture he kept, and whether he was keeping his garden tidy. And while she was there, she could retrieve some books Lord Malcolm had loaned him.

She took up his basket, trudged the path through the fields and woods, and when she arrived at the house was surprised to find herself surrounded by weeds, tares and brambles. The paint was peeling from the front door, and one of the window panes was cracked. Maybe he simply had not had the time to make the necessary repairs, and was busy with more important things. She knocked, listened and was shocked to hear the sounds of curses, and rising above the profanities, a soft woman's voice. A moment later, the door swung open and Hunt showed himself, his hair askew, his shirt unbuttoned and his face a-thunder.

When he saw Miss Watson, his demeanour changed like the sun changes the look of some angry mountain, and a lively twinkle burst into his eyes. "Oh," he said, "I thought I said there was no need for you to come to me."

"I…" she said, but the rest of whatever she was going to say stuck in her throat.

"And I should say, Miss Watson, that when I say something, I mean it. I stick to my word, and I expect others to do the same."

"Of course."

"So," he said, and now his voice suddenly turned black and edgy, "in future, simply leave the goods at your kitchen, as we agreed…"

Miss Watson took a box of eggs out of the basket and put them on the step. Then she unloaded a bag of beans, some apples, a bar of soap and a box of tea, stared back at Hunt and said, "And to think, when I met you I thought you were a gentleman."

"Miss Watson…" Now his voice was sinister, but before he had a chance to finish what he was going to say, she interrupted.

"And His Lordship has also asked me to retrieve his books."

"I haven't finished reading them," he said, wondering for a moment if he had met his match.

"His Lordship was most insistent."

"Well you can go home and tell your master, tell him… tell him to whistle for them."

"I think…"

"And if he can't whistle," said Hunt, and he pulled himself up to his full height and bared his teeth, "then he can blow a tune from his rear."

Now Miss Watson almost fainted. She had never, not in fifty-one years, been spoken to like that. She made a desperate, wheezing sound, forced herself to move, turned and walked down the path to the garden gate.

"Miss Watson!" he called, but she was not to be stopped. She carried on walking until she was out of sight, and then she started to run, up through the fields to the woods. When she reached the trees, she found she was weeping, something she had not done for many years. "Tears?" she said to herself. "Over him? Over a man?" – and at that moment, standing beneath an ancient oak with the thatched house behind her and Belmont in the valley below, she resolved to turn her face away from emotion and simply think about work, her cats and the careful monotony of a domestic life.

When Mr Prior-Stewart had finished telling the story of Miss Watson, I sat for a few minutes shaking my head. Things were a little clearer now, but still misty. I finished my cider, he finished his and pointed to his carriage. "I can drive you back to the house."

"No need," I said. "I think the exercise will do me good."

"It would be my pleasure," he said, and for a moment I caught a look in his eyes that I did not find comfortable.

"I think…" I said, but he caught my indecision and said, "In fact, I insist." So we said good afternoon to Mrs Beck and her dog, and I followed him back to the carriage and the lane to Ashbrittle.

The driver drove fast, and as we headed up the hill, Prior-Stewart and I did not talk, though there was a sharp, distinct atmosphere in the carriage. My feeling of unease grew when he let me out by the church and briefly put his hand on mine, squeezed it, leant towards me and said in a quiet and too familiar voice: "It was most pleasant to meet you. When I return to London, maybe we can arrange another meeting? I know of places…"

"Maybe," I said, but I had no intention of doing such a thing, or discovering what sort of "places" he was referring to. So I said a brief "goodbye" and walked the last half-mile to Belmont, and I sat in the cool of the library with the curtains drawn and the dark, silent masters of the French Enlightenment, and the pad of sad Miss Watson's cats in the hall.

My father was disappointed. When I left school I told him I wanted to go to Edinburgh University, but he did not understand my choice. I could not tell him I wanted to get as far away from Dover as possible, so I explained that I wanted to go to Scotland because the air was sweet and I wished to climb mountains, but he interrupted me with a lecture about the sort of people I would meet, the loose morals, the drink and the women. He sat behind his desk, and I sat in the chair normally reserved for troubled parishioners. After five minutes he tied himself in verbal knots, took a swift detour in memories of his own youth, got lost there, struggled back and with an exhausted sigh said, "Your mother would have been proud," and gave me an envelope containing a photograph of her, a five-pound note and a pen. Two months later he accompanied me to the railway station with my bags, shook my hand on the platform, turned and walked away. As I watched him go, he tucked his hands into his coat pockets and hunched his back against the wind that blew off the sea, through the town and into the station. I waited for him to turn and take a last look at me, but he did not stop, and for a moment I thought I would never see him again. I had a premonition of his death, but it was a false one, and after my first term I returned to Dover and he was still there, sitting behind his desk with a half-eaten digestive beside him, still causing merry hell with the ecclesiastical authorities.

I read History, and in my first year I accompanied three women to dances I did not enjoy, discovered a taste for Scottish beers, travelled to the highlands and climbed a dozen or more mountains, had an argument with my landlord about a damp wall and spent six weeks in bed with an unidentified illness. When I recovered, I was so far behind with my studies that I moved into the library and worked harder than I had ever worked before. I wrote a thousand words a day, revised them at night, wrote another thousand and revised again. I narrowed my eyes and focused on nothing but the Restoration and balance of European power in the seventeenth century. And when I had finished, I went to my favourite public house and met Timothy.

Timothy was reading Medicine, and our friendship was founded on the fact that we were both from Kent. We did not have much else in common. His father owned a shipping company, his mother was – by his account – a widow in all but name, and he had the look of a man who had never been loved. He had been raised by a stern governess, and neither of his parents had seen him take his first step. His first word had been "Eva" and his second word had been a German curse. "*Schwanz!*" he screamed when his father slapped him on the back of the legs for no good reason, and from that moment on, he dedicated himself to fighting his parents' will, opposing their wishes and proving he was stronger than fate.

He had been educated at boarding schools since the age of seven, and hid his intelligence behind nonsense and hyperbole. Within an hour of our first meeting, he told me there were only six people in the world who should wear deerstalkers, architects should pay twice as much tax as anyone else, and dog lovers should have to pass a detailed three-part exam before being allowed to keep a hound. But I did not think he believed what he was saying: his huge blue eyes gave him away, and I think he was simply voicing random ideas to see what effect they had. Because when I suggested he was talking nonsense, he did not stand his ground but went to the bar and ordered two more pints of the best beer.

He drank fast, smoked evil-smelling cigarettes and changed the subject. He told me his ambition was to write a novel, but was under pressure, too much pressure – pressure he had not asked for, did not want, could not cope with, wanted to take to a quarry and bury under a thousand tons of stone.

"What do you mean?"

"My brother went to Cambridge. He got a first, and Father's grooming him to take over the company. Edinburgh" – he lit another cigarette and waved it at nothing in particular – "they think I've failed already."

"I'm quite sure they think nothing of the sort."

"What makes you say that? Have you met my parents?"

"No, of course I haven't. I've only just met you." I looked at him, and for a moment I thought he was going to weep. His face creased at the edges, and he stared into his drink. I said, "Do you think you've failed?"

"No, but it doesn't matter what I think."

"You're fooling yourself."

"Do I look like I'm fooling myself?"

"Yes," I said.

He drank his beer in two gulps, said "I am not" and went to fetch another.

As he stood at the bar, he was surrounded by people who jostled and pushed around him, but he did not seem to notice them. He was tall but carried himself with a slight stoop, and as I watched him carry his drink back to the table, I saw a shadow pass across his eyes. He staggered and I thought he was going to drop the glass, but he did not. He managed to sit down, and as he stared at the glass, he said, "And what about you?"

"What about me?"

"What's your story?"

"It's nothing much," I said, but I told him anyway, and as he listened he nodded and agreed that Dover was a cold and windy town, and the castle smelt of cooked lentils.

And as I told him a story about getting lost in the castle and my father's voice echoing up a tower to me, he closed his eyes and fell asleep. He slept for about ten seconds, woke up with a jolt and said, "I was always getting lost." He picked up his beer and drank. "Always getting lost," he repeated, and I thought he was probably willing the state on himself, so in an effort to cheer his spirits, I changed the subject. I remember: I talked about travelling by train at night, and how loneliness is bred by the night and can freeze glass. He said he did not understand, and mumbled about hoping I knew what he meant. I said I did, and as I watched him slip into another ten-second nap, I thought, Timothy, I know exactly who you are.

What does the night do and how does it do it?

How do cats see in the dark and why do dogs howl at the stars?

Why do the shadows of the night snap so wildly, and what do rivers think as the black laps around their banks?

Does water recognize the signs of wind?

Do birds crouch and blink, and are the goblins firing their kilns, beating iron into knives and forks?

Who is leading a brindle calf to a clearing in the woods and tying it to a stake? And who are we, so lost in our own lies and imaginings?

And what are our lies and imaginings? Is one the lie of the idea that you can never change? The lie of a father's religious truth? The lie of one man's myths? And are the imaginings telling of a sweet and perfect love, one moored to a solid stone quay? One with sweet voices in the morning and the smell of woodsmoke drifting in still air?

And trees. Do trees see and hear, and when they are caught by the wind, do they talk to each other and compare thoughts? And when their leaves appear, do they feel pain? Do they know what they look like? Can they smell the dark? Can they feel the nails that pierce the guts of the men who walk in circles, around and around?

After supper I told Miss Watson I had work to do. I went back to the library. I worked for an hour but, for all its glory, the collection was losing its grip on me. Its fingers were slipping from my wrists, and my pen felt loose in my hand. My eyes started to glaze. I concentrated, but I still drifted. It was like this... the list of priceless books had grown to include a first of Diderot's *Pensées philosophiques* (scorch marks courtesy of the Parliament of Paris) and the 1797 three-volume edition of *Jacques le fataliste*. One volume of this novel would be a lucky find, two would be outrageous, but three… The pity was I did not care. I was thinking about something else. I noted the books' value and put them back on the shelf without a second thought.

At ten o'clock, Miss Watson poked her head around the door, said goodnight and told me not to work late. I heard her climb the stairs, cross the landing, go into her room, close the door and get ready for bed. The floor creaked and the water pipes grumbled. I waited twenty minutes. I stared at my fingernails for five minutes and listened to the house creak towards sleep. When I was sure she was asleep, I left the library, tiptoed down the hall, left the house by the kitchen door and crept into the night. I had a plan. I say a plan, but thinking back, I had no plan at all. All I had was my feet and my eyes, and a vague bundle of thoughts.

Amongst these thoughts was this one: Hunt was a persuasive liar, but not persuasive enough. I had found a reference to malaria in one of Lord Malcolm's books, and in addition to fevers, chills, headaches and jaundice, one of the symptoms of malaria was extreme lethargy. No mention of screaming and wailing, or scratching. Another thought was this: Hunt had unusually dark and mobile eyes. Another: maybe I should follow my instincts and keep my nose out of things that did not concern me, but another nagged, another told me that someone was in pain and trouble, and for once in my life I should step out of the safe and easy way.

The moon was swollen, and its full light gave the land a flat, endless look. The wood was a rash across the side of the hill, and the tops of the trees gashed the skyline. The cats were prowling and ran from me as I crossed the drive and jumped the gate into the orchard, and then I was under the apple trees and past the chicken coop. The hens scratched and rustled their wings. A fox was near. I smelt it, and as I turned my nose to the scent, I heard a howl. It cut a slice from the night and carried it away, buried it for later and ran ahead of me, across the fields and into the trees.

I was not afraid, but I was wary. I stopped every fifty yards to listen to the night, but heard nothing more than scurrying voles and wakeful birds as they flapped in the treetops. When I reached the woods I did not stop, and I climbed fast through the trees to the crest, and then I was down the other side of the hill and the lights of Hunt's house shone at me all the way.

Was I repeating myself?

Stop me.

Wait for me.

Please.

Am I repeating myself?

I do not know, but if I am, it is because my memories of this night are scrambled and twisted, and sometimes I believe my mind played – and is still playing – tricks on me. It decided what I should see and do and feel and smell before I saw or did anything, and left me stranded on the edge of what I believe and what could never be. Goblins in the woods? Mad people raking the world with wormwood? Stolen children in hidden houses? Trees that whisper and think? Of course I should have stayed away, but I did not know. I did not know what I was thinking.

When I got close to the house, I stopped and listened. I crouched behind the wall, touched the stones and wiped my fingers on my trousers. I was wearing a good pair of black trousers, a plain white shirt and a tweed jacket. I remember the jacket. And I remember I heard Hunt and a woman arguing. Malarial people do not argue. The voices rose and fell, and I stopped at the garden wall to listen. I did not understand a word, and as the argument continued I crept to the gate and stepped into the garden. The night caught the branches and leaves of the rambling plants and high grass, and their shadows played across the side of the house. I stopped behind a bush, and as I watched, I saw Hunt come to the window. He was holding a glass of whisky and smoking a cigarette. The smoke twirled up and clouded around his head. He stared out and clenched his fists. He did not look like the man I met before. A mask had dropped, and what I saw was his true face. It blazed and fought, and his mouth was curled into a thin, cruel wisp. He turned and disappeared, and the voices rose and fell.

I ducked down and skirted around the house to the back, and when I reached the kitchen door I leant against the wall and waited. I waited for a few minutes, the moon rose a degree and I decided to play it straight. I would knock on the door and demand to see whoever had been screaming, but before I had the chance, I heard the sound of glass shattering and a door slamming. I went to the corner of the house in time to see Hunt stalking through the garden to the front gate. He kicked it open and headed up the drive. He was holding a bottle, and when he reached the gate he stopped, yelled "Damn you!" at the sky and disappeared into the night. I waited for a few minutes and then returned to the kitchen door. I put my hand on the handle, rested it there for a moment, shut my eyes, took a deep breath and let myself into the house.

The heat was overwhelming and the air reeked of sweetness. The sink was piled with dirty plates and glasses. A bowl of rotting fruit sat in the middle of the table, and a broken chair stood in the corner. I stood and listened, but all I heard was the buzz of flies and the clang of motes as they drifted in the air. The rest was clammy silence, and this dropped its head on my shoulder and wrapped around me as if it had arms.

I left the kitchen and stepped into the hall. I was quiet. I slowed my breathing. I had a choice of three doors. Two were open and one was closed. I went to the first open one, put my head around it and looked into a sitting room. There was a mangy, broken settle in the middle of the floor, and a low table piled high with old newspapers. A vase of dead flowers stood on the window sill, and crooked pictures hung from the walls.

The next open door led into a room filled with boxes and tea chests, suitcases and carpet bags. There was a single bookshelf on the wall, and for a moment I thought about checking the spines, but I fought the impulse, stepped back into the hall and went to the closed door.

I put my hand on the handle, turned it and held my breath. The door opened with a slow, low squeak. The sweet smell was strong here. It wafted out and filled my head, and I put a hand over my nose before pushing the door wide and stepping into the room.

There was a doctor's couch in the middle of the room, steel and leather with wheeled feet and a white sheet folded at one end. Next to it was a glass-topped table with a row of silver instruments – scalpels, scissors, syringes and other things I could not identify – and a glass-fronted cabinet was standing against the wall. This contained a collection of bottles and boxes. I took a step towards it and, as I did, I heard a bedspring squeak above me, and the sound of a creaking floorboard. Then another floorboard, the click and turn of a door handle. A footstep on the landing, a second step, another floorboard, and someone started to come down the stairs.

They came hesitantly, and when they reached the bottom they stopped. They stood still and quiet. I took a single careful step backwards and stood behind the door, and as I waited, I heard the sound of slow breathing. I felt vague and light-headed, but did not care or think of an excuse for being there, so I stepped into the hall. As I did, I had one of those moments when time stops and twists, and the air contracts. My senses flared and tightened, and movement sharpened. There was no gap between what I knew and what I imagined, and no knots holding my thoughts together. All their strands fluttered out behind me, flags of things I had wondered, promised or wished. I closed my eyes tight and held them tight for a moment, took a breath and opened them again.

I was face to face with a small woman. I say face to face because I suppose it was like that, and I say small but she was only a little shorter than me, made shorter because she was crouching. She was trembling, too, and wearing a white cotton shift that reached halfway down her thighs. She had no hair on her head, and when I first saw her I thought her skin was beautifully painted. Really beautifully painted, carefully and perfectly with tiny brushes. Whoever had done it must have spent hours on the work, or days. Maybe even weeks. It was pale yellow with a pattern of brown blotches, and it shone and shadowed and glistened. Her eyes were huge – a deep, dark liquid brown. But as I looked more closely I realized that she was not painted, not painted at all. This was a tattoo, a brilliant tattoo made by a very patient artist, or if it was not a tattoo then she was wearing some kind of suit that mirrored her skin. Yes, I thought, a perfect – if scandalous – suit. She turned her head, and as she did she rustled lightly and bent towards me like I was the strange one and needed help. Her nose twitched, she rolled her eyes, she tipped her head back and sniffed the air. I took a step towards her, and as my right foot lifted off the ground and I moved my left to meet it, the truth dawned, broke over my head and sent me twisting. My blood flooded with heat. Every hair on my body froze. I opened my mouth. It was dry. I tried to blink, but it was impossible, because the truth was too awful. I tried to speak, but words were impossible. This woman was covered in scales, real, glistening scales. Only her eyes and nails were normal. The rest was spinning beyond me, spinning and twisting into a hole that gaped around me. Lost and gone. The chill flooded back and my brain snapped. I whispered, "Hee…" and the sound echoed in my head, "Hee…" it came back, like a bell across a deep, black valley.

She stared at me. I took another step towards her. As I did, she took a step backwards, balled her hands into fists and held them to her mouth. She made a little whining sound, and the hall candle twinkled over her skin. She took another jump backwards, she whined again and my head whined back, and I whispered, "Snakeskin."

She was covered in it. I say covered, but that is the wrong word. Her skin was it. She dropped her head. She rustled. It was getting hotter in that house, the sweet smell was getting sweeter and, as I struggled to breathe, a tear rolled from one of her eyes. She reached up and touched it onto the end of a finger. "Ahh…" she said.

I opened my mouth, but nothing came out.

"Plee…"

"Miss Hunt?" I said.

"Plee…"

"What?"

"Plee…"

"I'm sorry?"

"Plee…"

"Don't…" I whispered, "don't be… don't be scared." And as the words came out I thought, "Scared? You? Or me?" and my throat tightened, my mouth filled with salt and the chill was changed to heat. Sweat broke out across my forehead, ran down my face and dripped onto the floor. I fought with my legs. They wanted to run, but I would not let them. I would stay there shaking and they would obey me and I could not take my eyes off her skin. It was beautiful and so terrible, and I knew if I lived to be a thousand years old I would never erase it from my memory. It would stay there scorching and hurting until I died, and I would take my last breath with it branded on my eyes.

"Hurt," she said.

"You…"

"Hurt."

"Hunt?"

She shook her head.

"What's…"

"Plee…"

"What's happened to you?" I said. "Your…" I pointed, "skin…"

"Not…" Her voice was thin and wispy, as if it were bouncing through tissue paper.

"Not?"

"Mine…"

"God…"

"Yes."

"God…

95

"*Væ puto deus fio*," she said, and she dropped her head.

"What is that?"

"He says."

"Who?"

"Him," she said, and she looked down at her arms and she turned them over and stared at the patterns that covered them as if she was looking at them for the first time, and I thought her heart was about to break before me. Her eyes misted, her breathing quickened, her knees buckled and she started to crumple. I went to her and put my hands out, but she recoiled. "No!" she wailed. "Don't touch! Don't!" And I put my hands up, palms facing her and said "Please. Don't worry. I'm not going to hurt you."

She looked up at me, flicked out her tongue and licked her lips. Her eyes cleared and their colour brightened. "Worry?" she said, and for a moment I thought her mouth was going to twitch into a smile. But she dropped her head and I looked at the way the scales on her back turned from deep brown to yellow. They were beautiful and shiny, and the light caught them, held them and turned them over in its prism. When she looked back at me she said, "I saw you."

"Did you?"

"From the window."

"I'm working at the big house."

"I know," she said. "Hunt told. Called you the fool. The fool librarian."

"Did he?"

She nodded, took a deep breath and widened her eyes. She exhaled and I caught the sickly smell of her breath.

"I'm not a librarian," I started, but I did not finish.

"And I'm not... not Miss Hunt. I'm..." she did not finish the sentence.

"You're?"

She shook her head and whispered, "Can you... can you help me?"

There was no question.

"I have to go... get... get away..."

"Of course," I said.

"Now?"

"Yes," I said, but as I did, I heard a noise outside. I heard footsteps, cursing and the slam of the garden gate. She looked towards the sound, looked back at me and said, "Please..."

"Wait..." I said.

She stood up, took a step towards me and reached out a hand. "Please..." she said. The word snapped at me and I was trapped in front of her, my mouth hanging open and my own skin crawling with wonder and fear. I wanted to move but I could not, and when I tried to say something nothing came out. "Now?" she whispered.

Nothing.

"Please?"

"No..." I stammered. "No. Tomorrow."

"Tomorrow?"

"Yes."

"Tomorrow?"

"I'll come for you."

"You promise?" she said.

"I promise," I said.

"Or you die?"

"Or I die," I said, and then she began to climb the stairs. I said, "Stop…" and for a moment she did. She turned and looked back at me, raised her hand and held it to her head, but then she turned and disappeared around the corner and the front door was opening.

I hurried back down the hall to the kitchen, went to the back door and was outside again, and could hear Hunt inside. I ran into the garden and crouched in the long grass, and as I watched the house, the woman came to one of the upstairs windows and looked down at me. She put her right hand on the glass, tipped her head back and let out a high, desperate scream, and as she did, Hunt appeared behind her. He grabbed her arm, put a hand over her mouth and pulled her back. She tried to struggle, but did not have the strength. She disappeared and I heard a crash and the sound of breaking glass. A moment later the curtains were drawn, and then the house went quiet and I was left alone in the garden with the night birds and the insects who warred against the cracks of light.

I stood in the garden. My mind swirled. It twisted and dived between what I had seen and a nagging idea that what I had seen was not what I had seen and suns would collide in my belly before what I might have seen was what I had actually seen. But then I stopped this and turned, and started to walk back to Belmont. I started to walk and then I was going faster, and before I reached the woods I was running as fast as I could, and as I dashed through the trees, birds blew out of the branches and bushes and voles scurried down the track ahead of me. The low branches of the trees and bushes tried to grab me, and the exposed roots slashed at my feet. The leaves whispered my name, twigs broke away and rained on my head, and puddles and streams appeared where no puddles or streams had been before. I remembered Dante – *"Midway upon the journey of our life, I found myself within a forest dark, for the straightforward pathway had been lost..."* – and I forgot Dante and I remembered my father's constant caution. He would never have been as I was, caught between terror and flight on a warm, damp night. Never. He would have stayed at home with a book, a cup of tea and a biscuit. Biscuits, I thought, and I caught my foot in a rabbit hole, fell, pulled myself up and ran faster, down into the fields, up, through the orchard and onto the drive.

When I reached the house, I slammed the back door behind me and did not care how much noise I made as I climbed the stairs. I met the cats outside Miss Watson's room, and as I passed them they stood and arched their backs in alarm. "Go to sleep," I whispered, and they scurried away, along the corridor and downstairs to the kitchen.

When I reached my room, I lay on the bed, watched the moonlight pool on the floor and listened to the night. I heard Miss Watson's bed springs. I closed my eyes, but the dark

raised a vision of the woman in Hunt's house, so I opened
them again and tried to keep them open for as long as I could.
I do not know how long I managed – an hour, an hour and a
half – but I fell asleep eventually and, when I woke up, dull
sunlight was breaking through the window, and the chickens
in the orchard were scratching at worms and making the
lovely sounds busy chickens make.

In my second year at Edinburgh, Timothy and I decided to
share rooms. Like my room at Belmont, these rooms had a
view of an orchard, sunlight streamed in the windows and for
a month we had an easy time. He had resolved some of his
problems, his cynicism was on the wane, and he had decided
to tell his father he would never be interested in working for
the family firm, not at any time or cost. He was still drinking and smoking too much, but he had made a plan. He had
abandoned the idea to write a novel: when he graduated he
was going to "do some good in the world". He did not know
exactly how or where, but when he talked about it, his face
lost its forlorn look and his back straightened.

We were not inseparable, but we were close, so when I got
a call from the Royal Infirmary to say a Timothy Cash had
been admitted with serious injuries, I abandoned an essay
on the 1662 Act of Uniformity and walked to the hospital.

He had visited a public house where gown was not welcome, and after a few drinks had told someone that Edinburgh was full of people who did not know the difference
between stupidity and sense. Taken outside, led into a side

alley and beaten with fists, bottles and a bar stool, he had lost two pints of blood and suffered three broken ribs, a broken arm and a crack in his skull.

As I sat beside him and listened to the physicians confer, a nurse told me he was a lucky man. She mopped his brow and listened to his pulse. He did not look lucky. His head was swathed in bandages, his eyes were black, and as he slept, I resolved to make sure he straightened out and found new ways to express himself. I stayed with him for a couple of hours and went back to see him the next day. He was still in a bad way but was sitting up, and when I arrived he already had a pair of visitors. He introduced them as his mother and father. Polished and angry-looking people, they looked at me as if I was exactly the sort of person they did not want their son to know, and who was probably responsible for his current state. But when he explained I was his only friend, and if he had not met me he would have been the loneliest student in Edinburgh, they offered me grudging thanks. I fetched a chair, but before I could sit down, his father stood up and said they had important family matters to discuss. "Business…" he said, and I said "Of course", as if I knew what he was talking about. Timothy looked at me, and although he did not say anything, his eyes shone with need and anguish. I hesitated and, as I did, his father held out his hand and said, "It was a pleasure to meet you."

"Yes," I said to him and, "I'll call tomorrow" to Timothy, but when I went back in the morning, his bed was occupied by a small bald man with an enormous bandage over his left eye and his arm in a sling. A nurse told me Timothy had been moved to a private hospital in Canterbury.

"Canterbury?"

"Yes."

"Why?"

The nurse did not know, so when I got home I finished my essay and handed it in with an apologetic note. I caught a railway train in the morning, and was in Dover by midnight.

My father was astonished to see me, and after admonishing me for waking him up, told me to help myself to cocoa and go to bed before I fell asleep on my feet. I did as I was told, and in the morning, after an awkward breakfast in a very cold kitchen, I went to see Timothy.

He was as astonished to see me as my father had been, and after rebuking himself for being weak and foolish, and saying some unkind things about his parents, he managed a smile and thanked me for visiting. "I don't think I've had a real friend before," he said, and for a moment I thought his face was going to collapse. It began to fail around the edges like a ridge of sand is washed clean by the tide, but he pulled back, sat up and flicked some crumbs off his blanket.

"You must have."

He shook his head. "My father used to frighten them."

"You should meet mine," I said, and we laughed.

I stayed for half an hour, and we talked about fathers, university and drinking, and when I left I made him promise to come back to Edinburgh as soon as he was feeling well enough.

At the time, I remember thinking this was probably the last time I would see Timothy, so when I saw him a month later, I was surprised. He was emerging from a lecture hall, books under his arm with clear eyes, a neat haircut and a wide smile. I have no idea what had happened to him, or how, but when I spoke to him it was as though he had had a religious conversion and saw life as a pure challenge to a pure mind and a pure body. I offered to buy him a drink, but he turned me down, and laughed when I suggested a glass or two of port.

"I'm past all that," he said, and there was not a trace of smugness in his voice, or doubt.

I waited for him to slip back to his old ways, but he did not. I waited for a message from a public house or a hospital, but it never came, and although we met each other a few times, the changed Timothy dedicated his final year to solid study, and while I worked inexorably towards my average degree, he found himself with a first and the unqualified approbation of his parents.

When I went down for breakfast, Miss Watson was waiting for me. She had a face like a storm, and her hair was sticking up like a twigs on a blown bush. She slammed the teapot down on the kitchen table and said, "Sometimes I wonder if you give other people a second thought."

"Miss Watson," I said.

"Yes?"

"Do you know what Professor Hunt does over there?"

"Why? What has that man got to do with the noise you were making last night? I had no idea what to think. I thought I was going to be attacked, and when you…"

"I visited him last night, and there's no case of malaria in his house. Far from it…" I said, but then I stopped. Miss Watson was not going to believe a word I said. She shook her head.

"You visited him again? I don't believe it."

"I'm afraid so."

"I'm beginning to think," she said, "that the sooner you're away from here the better."

"I'll be leaving today," I said. "I've a couple of hours' work to do, and then I'm finished."

She did not bat an eye.

"So…" I said, trying to be firm, "maybe you could tell me where I could hire a carriage."

"A carriage?" Her scornful look could have melted iron.

"Yes."

"I believe Mr Wilkinson has a dog cart, but whether it's for hire, well…"

"And he lives where?"

"Raymond's Farm. At the crossroads."

"And he has a horse?"

"A cart without a horse would be of little use," she said, but I ignored her sarcasm, stood up and returned to the library. I sat with the books, the portrait and the bust, and knew I had to be strong. I was trapped between reason and magic, Voltaire and someone I imagined was called Hunt, Belmont and a thatched house that probably did not exist. I tried to believe this, tried to force myself into a cupboard I could not lock, but I knew I was fooling myself. I knew what I had seen. I had not been dreaming. I was on solid ground, the solid ground of the strength of reason. So I went back to work, and by midday I had listed the last volumes and initialled the last index sheet. I filed my papers, tidied Buff-Orpington's desk and stood in front of the bookcases for one last time.

When I arrived at Belmont, I had been overwhelmed by the collection, but now I did not care and, when I closed the library door for the last time, did not feel any sense of regret. My head was swamped and damp, agitated birds were picking at my brain. I went upstairs, packed my bags, left them in the hallway and walked away from the house, up the lane to the village. I found Mr Wilkinson of Raymond's Farm. He had a look of complete desolation on his face. His sheep were dead, his cattle were ulcerated and hobbled, his crops were rotting in the desperate fields. He was sitting in his kitchen with a mug of cider at his elbow – I say kitchen, but with its dirt floor, empty cupboards and crooked table, it was more of a barn. The air was thick with a rank, dead smell, and clouds of flies swarmed over the filthy windows. A scrawny dog was lying on the floor. Too weak to lift its head towards me, let alone bark, it was suffering from terrible sores on its back. So when I offered a good sum for the hire of his horse and cart, with the promise I would leave it in the care of the drivers at Taunton railway station, he almost smiled, and thanked me with embarrassing intimacy, hugging and patting my back as though I was a long-lost son. "Just don't drive him too hard," he said. "He's not as strong as he used to be."

The bells fell silent. The bells rang again. My father lost his battle of the bells and spent the last period of his working life waging a more subtle war of attrition against the ecclesiastical authorities. They knew he was due to retire within a couple of years, so they humoured him and conceded a few minor points on floral displays. But while the bells rang in the tower above him, he felt he was being mocked. When I returned to Dover for the Christmas of my final year, the vicarage was freezing and there was no life in the place. No tirades against the mediocrities who had crawled their way to the top. No rage at the congregations who had turned their back on his church and flocked to the chapel down the road. And no attacks on the toothless academics who were teaching me nothing but nonsense. For the first time in my life, I thought he was beaten. His back was hunched, his eyes were washed and pale, and he looked as if he had lost six inches in height. On Christmas morning, I gave him a biography of Lord Nelson and he gave me a book of engravings of Scotland. Then he went out to take the morning carol service, and, as he left, he turned to me and said, "I have some news."

"What news?"

"I'll tell you later."

I did not go to church, so I went down to the front and stood to watch the ships in the harbour. Gulls swooped and cried, weak waves lapped against the breakwaters, and when

I walked back I was overwhelmed by a feeling of imminent loss. I do not know where this feeling came from, and when I reached St Michael's I sat on the wall outside and listened to the last carol. I watched the congregation leave, nodded to a few people I knew from years ago, and then joined my father in the vestry.

As he hung his surplice in the wardrobe, he said, "This is my last Christmas here. I'm retiring in the spring."

"I thought you had a few more years."

"So did I, but I've decided to leave before I do something foolish."

"Foolish?"

"Yes," he said. "I think you know what I mean." I looked into his eyes. He was being serious. Then he turned away, closed the wardrobe and left by the side door. I followed, and we walked back to the vicarage together, up the hill and around the corner.

When we got inside, I helped him with his coat and made him sit in the kitchen and took out a bottle of sherry. I poured two glasses and held mine up. "Happy Christmas, Father."

He ran his finger round the top of the glass and allowed a smile to creep across his face. "Yes," he said. "Happy Christmas, David," and after we had chinked our glasses, he downed his in one gulp. He poured himself another, and while I stared wide-eyed at this display – I had never seen him drink more than half a glass of sherry at a sitting – he took a deep breath, stood up, paced the room twice, sat down again and told me the story of his life. I had not expected it or asked for it, and some of the things he said came as a shock, but once he had started he did not – or could not – stop.

He was born in Southampton. This much I already knew. His father worked in the docks, drank heavily, came home late and beat his mother. He had an elder brother and a younger sister, and they lived in a ruined house in the poorest quarter of the city.

My father did not do well at school. He refused to study and preferred to spend his time bullying other children, learning how to smoke and throwing stones at dogs. By the time he was sixteen, he was the leader of a gang of boys who terrorized his neighbours. By his own admission, he was fortunate to survive this period of his life unscathed and out of prison, for he pickpocketed, robbed houses and caused all manner of nuisance. Until one night, while lying in bed, a blinding light filled the room and Christ appeared in a cloud. The Son of God stretched out his arms, and while a host of cherubim and seraphim swarmed around his head, he called my father's name – "George... George..." – and told him there was work to be done. So in the morning my father was a new man, glowing with the light of Christ and anxious to redeem himself.

He renounced his old friends, enrolled in night school and studied for the exams he had missed. By this time, his own father had drunk himself to death and his elder brother had moved out, so he took responsibility for his mother and younger sister, and took work in the docks.

He worked hard, studied harder, fell asleep at his desk, went to church every Sunday, and by the time he was twenty-one had been accepted by the Society of the Lord's Sacred Mission to study for the Anglican priesthood. A celibate and monastic group, the Society were strict and taught my father well, and though he argued with them about some aspects of interpretation and teaching, when he left the mission it was with a heavy heart.

He worked as a curate in Northampton before his appointment as parish priest of St Michael's in Dover. Within a year he had met my mother, and spent an anxious six months trying to come to terms with his attraction. Her name was Josephine Ray, she was pale and shy, and she worked in the Bishop's office. She had a quiet faith and a gentle manner, and after months of prayer and meditation, he renounced his vow of celibacy and announced his intention to marry. Maybe this is where my father's straightened life derailed itself and uncertainty – and guilt – started to creep back in. There are only so many changes one man can cope with, and maybe he took change to its limits, and maybe this is why my thoughts of him are so coloured by fear and worry.

The woods were quiet. A shower of rain had fallen, and the leaves and branches were dripping. The air was damp but not weak with it: it was tight like a fist. I stood the cart in front of Belmont, gave the horse a nosebag, and loaded my bags. Now I walked away from the house quickly, my head down, my feet quiet. When I reached the place where I had first met Professor Hunt, I stopped and sat beneath a beech tree. I leant against the trunk, closed my eyes, opened them again and felt an ant climbing up my arm. I brushed it off. Clouds were low and threatening. Flies buzzed in the air. I listened to my heart beat and watched the thatched house where she was kept. I watched the windows and I watched the weeds in the garden, and the hedge that snaked around the front. The overgrown apple trees. A broken-down shed. I watched until the front door opened and Hunt appeared.

He stood on the step, shaded his eyes and stared at the sun, then stared in my direction and patted his jacket pockets. He went back indoors and emerged a minute later with a walking stick. He crossed the drive, slashed his way through the garden and took one of the winding paths that crossed the fields. I left the shade of my tree and scuttled into the woods, headed back along the ridge and reached a point where the trees thinned into scrub and the land dipped towards the west.

I watched him for a couple of minutes. He stopped, bent down and stared at a flower. He picked it, held it to his nose and rolled it between his fingers before tossing it away. He turned his back to me and strolled in the opposite direction. When he had disappeared, I stepped out of the woods, ran to a hedge, ducked down, waited, ran another fifty yards and stopped at a gateway. The gate was hanging off its hinges, and hundreds of lengths of string were draped over one of the posts. I stopped, listened and watched the house. It was quiet and still, the chimney smoking. I started running again, down the hill, over the low wall, through the back garden and up to the kitchen door.

I caught my breath and listened. I heard nothing. I tapped on the door and tried the handle, but it did not move. I waited a minute, but there was no answer, so I banged harder, crouched down and tried to look through the keyhole. I saw nothing, but a moment later I heard her calling.

"Help!"

"Hello!" I called.

"In here!"

I took a few steps back and aimed a kick at the door. It did not move. I kicked again. It cracked. One more kick and it splintered and swung open. I ran through the kitchen, tripped over a stool, stood in the hall and called "Hello!" again.

"I'm in here!" She was shouting from the room with the couch and the instruments. I had to kick another door to reach her, and when I saw her I retched. She was tied to the couch with leather straps. She turned her head towards me. Her cheeks were covered in tears. "You came..." she mumbled. Her voice had a crackle to it, ice cracking across a thawing lake, geese flying to breeding grounds, paint peeling off the hull of a beached boat. A fly buzzed and a window pane rattled.

I rushed to her and started to undo the straps around her ankles. The scales there were worn and sore, weeping yellow pus and blood. "Of course I did," I said.

"Thank you... thank you..."

"Ssh..."

I moved to her wrists, and as I was freeing them I heard a noise upstairs. I looked at the ceiling, froze, and she whispered, "Mice…" The noise came again, and the scrabbling of tiny feet. I undid the last strap, she took a shallow breath and moved her legs off the couch. She grimaced, then pointed to her dress, hanging on the back of the door. I fetched it and dropped it over her head. She arranged the straps on her shoulders, stood up, and the dress fell down over her stomach and legs. She lifted a cowled cape from the back of the door, wrapped it over the dress, covered her head and said, "We'll need that." She pointed at a black bag. I picked it up and said, "Anything else?"

"My shoes are at the door." She stepped towards me and I put my hand on her shoulder. She winced, but did not pull away.

"Can you walk?"

"How far?"

"Over the hill."

She looked at me and did not blink. "Show me," she said, and we went to the back door. As she laced her shoes, I stared out and listened. I pointed to the east, beyond the garden wall. "I saw him go that way," I said.

"That's where he likes to walk."

"How long does he go out for?"

"It depends," she said.

"On what?"

"How he's feeling. Sometimes he's gone for hours, other times he's back in twenty minutes."

"Then we leave now," I said, and I stepped out of the house. I stood in the shadow of the back door, looked both ways and beckoned her out. At first she would not move and stood absolutely still, watching the clouds. Her face looked out from under the cowl like something from the very worst dream, a dream a madman might have in the desperate last minutes of night, before the dawn comes and breaks the spell and chases all madness away. But do not stay, madness. Fly away. Leave. I wanted to shout at her but went back instead, took her arm and pulled her away from the house. When we reached the garden wall I let go, stopped and said, "Are you sure about this?" She gave me a short, hateful look, then started running.

We darted out of the garden and into the fields, and once we were away from the house, she moved quickly. We followed the line of the hedge, and when we reached the scrub below the woods, I stopped, she stopped behind me and I watched for Hunt. I saw nothing, so we carried on, up the hill and into the trees, but as we ran along the crest, I saw a movement in front of us, the flash of an unnatural green against the rest, and the noise of heavy steps. "Down," I hissed, and we dived for cover in a hollow below the track. Hunt was coming towards us, slashing at the undergrowth with his stick and muttering to himself. As he got closer, I heard his heavy breathing. It had a rattle to it, coming from the back of his throat. He said, "Now they will listen…" and then suddenly, before he reached where we were hiding, he stopped. I reached back and put my hand over the woman's mouth, and my legs started to tingle. I looked down at my feet. They were resting on leaves and twigs. He was about twenty-five feet away, and although his face was wearing the shrewd mask he had worn when I first met him, now I could see the mendacity in his eyes. Everything about him howled of a mad but perfect duality. He spoke again, this time something I did not understand, then turned around and walked back the way he had come. I waited a minute, stood up and watched his back disappearing through the trees, and then we carried on through the woods and down the track to the fields in front of Belmont.

The dog cart was where I had left it, and the horse was looking tired. It had finished the nosebag and was swishing its tail in a bored, distracted way. I took the woman's hand and said, "Now we run" – and so we did, through the orchard and the gate to the drive. Chickens flapped, the cats jumped off a wall, rooks burst from the castellations. I looked up and saw Miss Watson. She was upstairs, looking out of the landing window. When she saw me she raised her hand to wave, but then stopped, her arm frozen over her head, the colour draining from her face. She disappeared, we carried on running and were on the drive before she came running from the house shouting, "Stop! Mr Morris! Please!" She was almost pleading, and her face was lost in a look I hadn't seen before. I think she was worried, scared or panicked, or all three. But her jaw dropped as she saw the woman who stood beside me, shining yellow and brown with a wince on her face and her huge eyes staring out from beneath her cowl.

For a moment, I thought about turning and going to Miss Watson and explaining something, but what, and where to start? Where to end? Did the story have an end? Could it? I did not have the hours I would need, so I yelled "I'm sorry!" and helped the woman into her seat, tucked her cloak around her, pulled the nosebag off the horse, jumped into the driver's seat, released the brake, flicked the reins, and away we were up the drive towards the village. I raised my hand and held it up as we drove away, and the woman beside me started to whimper, and as we disappeared around the first bend of the drive, Miss Watson's desperate voice faded in the damp, sick air.

London

I used to be a book valuer. I was employed by an auction house and I lived in London. My beautiful, spacious rooms were at the top of a converted Georgian house overlooking Highbury Fields. My sitting room had white walls and was lined with bookshelves. Three old prints of Edinburgh hung between the two bay windows, and a watercolour of the Norfolk marshes hung over the fireplace. I had a comfortable settle and a blue armchair, and a collection of treasures and souvenirs on the mantelpiece.

My bedroom was dark, and besides a bed, a dressing table and a wardrobe, the room was filled with more books. The kitchen overlooked the backs of the gardens of the neighbouring houses, and the bathroom was painted green. I had polished the hall floorboards and covered them with patterned rugs from the orient.

I loved my rooms. When I came home from the office, I used to relax on the settle with a glass of sherry, close my eyes and let the day sink into the floor. It was wonderful to sit at the kitchen table in the summer and watch the evening light splinter through the trees, and know the clip and rumble of the city meant nothing. I was secure in my life, sheltered in the knowledge of reason, happy with my own company and my work. Pleased. This is a word you could have used to describe me.

I was back in touch with Timothy. He was living nearby, working for a good firm of solicitors, and when we met for a drink he did not betray his fractured and unhappy past. The change had stuck, and he said he was happy in his work. I did not believe him. There was a crease in his voice when he told me he was happy, but I ignored it. There was nothing I could do.

My father, retired from the church and living in a small house by the river in Canterbury, was changing. He was reading the sort of literature he used to avoid – Ovid, Chaucer and Shakespeare's poetry – and even visiting the theatre to enjoy opera, a musical form he used to believe was more dangerous than any other. His new interests showed themselves in brighter eyes than I had seen before, clear skin and a straightened back. "We shall not all sleep," as Paul wrote to the Corinthians and my father quoted to me before I left to value the Buff-Orpington Collection, his finger wagging and his eyes lit with the memory of a different faith, "but we shall all be changed."

When we arrived at my rooms, the woman with snakeskin was weeping, shivering and hugging her coat to her neck. The journey from Somerset had not been easy, but it had been smooth, and although the railway carriage was crowded, I had managed to secure a private compartment by informing the guard that my companion was feverish and needed quiet and privacy. Once she had settled she had slept, and now she stood in the hall and the tears rolled down her face, and when I asked her if she wanted anything she said, "I must have it hot. Very hot." I fetched blankets, wrapped them around her, carried her to my bed and watched for five minutes. The shivering slowed, then she made little snoring sounds, like a mouse trapped in a box. I left her with the door open, lit all the fires, checked on her once more, poured myself a large glass of sherry and went to the sitting room.

I lay on the settle, stared at the ceiling and the floor, studied the pictures of Edinburgh and drifted into a light sleep. Dreams came, pleasant ones about walks over moors and along beaches, and one where I was walking with a woman I knew when I was living in Scotland. Her name was Grace, and she was very beautiful and studious, her fair hair was like an unusual plate of food, and the flights of freckles on her face were signposts to another life. Everything was very clear, like I was dreaming through glass.

It was like this: we had taken a weekend in her cousin's house at Sandwood Bay, in the far north-west. The sea was blue and fierce and crashed around the stack at the far end of the shore. The grass rustled in the dunes and the terrible ghost who was meant to walk the sands was watching us from behind the walls of a ruined croft. With his Polish face and his Polish boats and the seaweed hanging from his shoulders, he dashed against the rocks after drowning in a gale. Blood ran from his face, his eyes were white and his hair was covered in barnacles. His dead brain was filled with frozen memories of Gdańsk, amber and shattered rigging, and the climb through a tower to the cathedral roof where he proposed to a dark-eyed woman he never saw again. Grace was spooked and wanted to leave. She said she had heard a voice in her ear, whispering words she did not understand. The sand was hard and ridged, and there were gulls in the sky. They were crying and singing songs to each other, and when I awoke their songs were still in my head. I turned over and rubbed my eyes. The dream had not felt like a dream, but it had been. I had not been at Sandwood Bay with Grace and a Polish ghost. I had been in bed, in London, asleep. I stood up, went to the bathroom and splashed water on my face. The fires were roaring. I went to the kitchen.

The woman with snakeskin was standing by the table, looking out of the window. She was naked, drinking a glass of water, and her skin was shining. She turned to face me. We stood and stared at each other.

I was struck dumb.

She whispered, "London…"

I nodded.

"London…"

My mouth was tight: the words stuck. I forced one. "Yes," I said.

"I'm in London."

The early-evening sun glanced off her scales, and although it was impossible not to gawp at her in amazement, it was a frightening and disorientating thing to do, and made me want to sit down.

I said, "I'm sorry." Sweat was pouring down my face. I took out a handkerchief and wiped my eyes.

"Why?"

"For staring."

"No," she said, "stare." And she stepped away from the table, spread her arms like wings, dropped them, raised them again and slowly turned around.

How can I describe what stood before me? What can I write? Did reason collapse at that moment, turn and run through the marshes? Did the bitterns stab my heart with their beaks? Was I dreaming? And, I wondered, are books enough? Books sleep, awake, open, and sometimes even change a life. They move like herds of animals across dust plains and leave clouds in the sky. What can I say? Could music help? Some strange piece of courtly music, played by ancient men for another ancient man who, with a nod of his hand, could have the musician's cut fingers in a jar. I speak for myself when I write, and do not worry about the consequences, the reasons or the meaning. These things are for people who think they understand or know. I stared at her and, as I did, I turned the vision in my head like a ball, turning and turning and turning until the sight began to make sense.

This was the first time I had seen her in good light and as she moved, the yellow scales darted spots over the walls and ceiling, and the brown patches deepened their colour. These were spaced irregularly down her arms, thighs and calves. She had an oblong of brown around one of her breasts but not the other, and a single patch in the middle of her stomach. The scales grew smaller and blackened as they narrowed towards her groin. Her back was mainly brown, but where the scales tapered to her neck, a thin line of yellow broke through. Her head was mostly a darker yellow than the rest, with a brown oblong across her forehead, a crescent shape on her crown and a line that ran from the corner of each eye to the corners of her mouth. The skin around her wrists and ankles was paler than the rest, but the pus and blood from her wounds had dried. Her hands and feet were completely brown, and there were little whorls of scales around her ears. She stroked her arms. Her eyes were huge and shone with tears. She smelt of sugar, and when she moved she rasped.

"It is…" I began, but then I stopped.

"What?"

"No."

She narrowed her eyes. "Tell me."

I shook my head. "How can I?"

"Beautiful?" she said. "Is it beautiful?"

"Yes," I said. "It is miraculous. Awful. Amazing."

"I know," she said, and she sat down again. She put her hands out and laid them on the table.

I said, "Can I touch?"

She turned her head away.

"Please?" I said.

"Why?"

"Because I want to."

A silence dropped, lifted and hovered in the air. It looked down at us for a minute with a single clear blue eye, and as it did she stretched out her right arm. It came to me slowly, rustling across the table, the fingers pulling it. I shuddered, and then I took it and turned it over in mine. It was cool, dry and perfect, and when her fingers reached around and gripped, the keels of the scales left marks on me. I whispered, "Everything that comes out of the hands of the Creator of all things is good…"

"Excuse me?"

"…and everything degenerates in the hands of man."

"What are you saying?"

"Rousseau," I said, like a fool.

"Oh…"

"And can I ask you…"

"What?"

"What is your name?"

"My name?" Her voice cracked.

"Yes."

"My name is Isabel."

"Isabel…"

"Isabel Carter."

Isabel Carter. This is a beautiful, chiming name. To me, it sounds like a kind of rose, a rare thing, picked and placed carefully in a perfect vase. A scarlet rose with a tight heart and flared petals.

She was born in Charmouth, a village on the Dorset coast. Houses run down a hill to a bridge over a river, and lanes wind towards the sea. There are a few shops and public houses. It is a pretty place with walks along the beach and over the cliffs, and the air is salty fresh. Isabel's father was a physician, her mother was inclined to write poetry, and she had an older brother called Simon. She enjoyed a safe, happy childhood, like something out of a story for children. The family home was big and bright. It had tall windows and ceilings, and a walled garden. It was a five-minute walk from the beach, and if you strolled in the other direction, the lanes led to hedged fields and tracks that climbed to ancient wooded hill forts.

She developed a fascination for palaeontology and spent hours hunting for fossils along the shore. Solitary and happy with her own company, she walked out in all weathers, and when storms battered the coast and the cliffs collapsed onto the beach, she climbed over the mud slides and filled a canvas bag with ammonites, belemnites and shards of fossilized fish. This passion grew to embrace the science of living things, and when she was asked, at the age of twelve, what she wanted for Christmas, she said, "A hammer."

She was a brilliant pupil at a fine school, but when she announced she was going to be a famous scientist, she was told to be realistic and not such a dreamer. But she had made an irrevocable decision and would use her skills to develop cures for the worst ailments. Her grandmother suffered from an incurable disease that wasted her brain and erased her memories, and when she visited her in her room at the far end of the upstairs corridor, she told her that one day no one would need to suffer from disease. Once, her grandmother had worked as a missionary nurse in Africa. She had worked in hospitals where insects the size of plates scuttled across her face at night, honey was a balm and leaves were used as plasters. She had helped to establish a maternity hospital on the Gold Coast, but now she could not remember where the Gold Coast was or what maternity was or who this girl was, and she would ask her when her clever grand-daughter was going to visit, because she always did and never forgot.

When Isabel Carter left school, she was determined to continue her career in the sciences, and although her father and mother tried to convince her that a career in nursing was the only appropriate work for a woman of her character and inclinations, she chose to travel to Cambridge. She carried a letter of introduction from the headmistress of her school to a Professor of Biology at Downing College who – she had heard – was looking for an assistant who possessed understanding, patience and meticulousness. His name was Professor Richard Hunt. At that time he was a gregarious and ambitious man, even charming. His guile and cunning had yet to show, but his mendacity was already well formed. He told Isabel he had a dream. No, he would not tell her what it was, she would have to wait, and although he did not say so, she knew that if she earned his respect and trust, one day he would confide in her. She knew this instinctively, like a gorging ortolan in its locked box knows about the light and air outside, and imagines it under its wings.

She found rooms in a house on Emmanuel Road, and although she had opportunities to meet new friends, as the child, so the woman – and she preferred to keep her own company. She took her work very seriously and did not want distractions, and as she sat up in the night and tried to understand Professor Hunt's research, she thought of her grandmother sitting in Charmouth. The windows rattled and the sea broke along the shore, and millions of tons of sand and gravel were hauled by the tides. The land was turned to sea. Birds failed in flight and fish slipped away.

If she was asked exactly what the Professor was working on, she would not have been able to explain, but she would have said it was important and certain to result in great benefit to mankind. For the man was as close to a genius as she had ever met, and when one day he suggested they leave the laboratory early and take tea in a little shop he knew, she felt limp with excitement. He said he had matters to explain and he felt – looking into her eyes and smiling slightly – she would understand.

They sat at a corner table, and he ordered Earl Grey and a plate of rich cakes. After five minutes of weather talk, he leant towards her and said he was doing some independent research, research the college knew nothing about. He trusted her and hoped, even believed, that she trusted him. In return for a modest increase in salary and her total discretion, would she be interested in helping him with this work?

She was speechless. "Interested?" she said.

"Yes."

She looked into his eyes and searched for a trick, a mistake, a lie, but saw nothing like that, nothing dangerous or malignant at all. Just intelligence, perceptiveness and conviction. She believed him completely, and when she said "Why me?" he reached across the table and said, "Because you're the most gifted assistant I've ever had." She believed him again, believed him like flood comes to a river or the rain to earth, and his words seeped beneath her skin. She felt a flush in her blood, a blush in her cheeks and she looked away. He leant towards her and touched her hand. His fingers were ice-cold, but she did not shiver. She knew as he knew, and when he pulled his hand away and sat back, she was already with him, willing and honoured to work for the most brilliant man she had ever met.

Before the Professor introduced her to his mysterious research, he suggested she take a holiday, so she travelled home to Charmouth for a week. She walked along the beach, climbed the cliffs and wandered into the fields behind the village. She climbed the ramparts of the old hill fort where Egbert the Great had received emissaries from East Anglia, Mercia and Northumbria, and she remembered the stories she had been taught at school. The cruel Danes had ravaged the north and east of the country, and were threatening to land their ships at Charmouth. The King had called a council of war. For the first time in history, the kingdoms of England joined together to fight a common enemy. A common enemy, a field of blood, ships as far as the eye could see. Isabel sat with a view of the village and the sea, ate an apple and thought about her future.

She thought carefully, made a decision, and when she was sure she was doing the right thing, she went home to sit with her grandmother. The old lady sat in a huge armchair, stared at her granddaughter and told her that Isabel was such a lovely girl, with her huge eyes and her curly brown hair. "She is always visiting, and if you stay for a while, maybe you will meet her. You cannot miss Isabel Carter. She will be smiling and will tell you about the ichthyosaur bones she found a few years ago. Or maybe she will have her head in a book and you must not disturb her. Not when she is studying. Ssh. You must be quiet in the room."

Ten months before I met her, Isabel left Charmouth, moved back to Cambridge and started work on Professor Hunt's new research. She took her old rooms on Emmanuel Street, but after a couple of weeks Hunt said it was ridiculous: he had more than enough room in his own house, and would be happy to let her live in the empty servants' quarters. "Would it be proper?" she said, and when he said, "I don't know why not," she moved in. And at that time, as autumn collapsed over the city and she stared from her window at the overgrown garden below, she thought she knew satisfaction and purpose and all

the things she had promised her grandmother were waiting for her.

She sat at the table with her back to the window, and I sat
opposite. The sun was sinking through the trees, and the
sound of laughing children drifted from Highbury Fields.

"What happened to you?"

"Professor Hunt." She stared at her fingers. "He happened
to me."

"How?"

She shrugged, as if nothing could have prevented the
inevitable. Dreams, nightmares – they did not exist for
her any more. She shrugged again and ran her fingers
over the top of her head. She rubbed a scale, rolled
her eyes and said "Because I thought..." but her voice
dropped away, like a stone falling into a well. I waited
for her to finish what she was going to say, but when
she did not, I leant across the table and said, "Why did
you let him do it?"

"I didn't!" She glared now, her eyes bulged, and little spots
of spittle appeared at the corners of her mouth. "I didn't let
him do anything! This isn't my fault! I had no idea..."

"I'm sorry..."

"So am I."

"And... and it is snakeskin?"

"Yes."

"Really snakeskin?"

"Yes."

"It's difficult to believe."

"Oh, you can believe," she said, and she held up her hand. "It's from the fox snake."

"The fox…"

"Snake."

"Snake…"

"They live in the Americas."

"And it's yours, not just grafted or…"

"This is my skin."

"God."

"Mine."

"How did he do it?"

"I don't know."

"No?"

"I have my own ideas, but I can't be sure they have anything to do with what really happened."

"So he wasn't working on a cure that would benefit all mankind?"

She shook her head. "Of course not. He lied to me," she said. "I believed him once, but now…"

"What?"

"I thought he was a genius. Really. Not just a clever man, someone more than that."

I nodded.

"It's difficult to explain, but he had discovered a way of fooling human cells into thinking they were doing one thing when they were actually doing something else. It's a form of metastasis. A corrupt form, but nevertheless…"

She sipped some water. Her lips were covered in the finest yellow scales, and when she touched the glass to them, she squinted.

"And this is the result."

"As simple as that?"

"Simple," she said, "is not a word I would use. Think. You take a group of cells, introduce them to an environment designed to reject invasion and expect the cells to survive. It sounds impossible, *is* impossible, but if you…"

"Stop!" I stood up, drank a glass of water, gulped it, drank another and sat down again. "Stop!"

She dropped her head and sniffed. "Why? You asked the question."

"I'm lost already."

"Lost?"

"Yes," I said. "I'm books. Literature. I was useless at science."

She sipped some more water. "I love the sciences…"

"How long have you been…"

"How long have I been what?"

I pointed at her face. "Like this."

"Six months."

"Why? Why did he do it?"

"I have no idea. I think he'd been ridiculed and wanted revenge. He'd written about his ideas, but no one would publish them. His colleagues thought he was mad, so he decided to prove them wrong."

"God."

"Hell. And why you?"

She shrugged. "There was a time when he could have done whatever he wanted with me. I'd have walked on hot coals, put needles in my eyes, anything..."

"You were in love with him?"

"Maybe," she said. "Once, in a strange way..." and she reached up and ran her right hand down her left arm. "A very strange way..."

I drank some more water, ran my finger around the rim of the glass and said, "What does it feel like?"

She turned her head. The scales around her eyes caught the light and shimmered. "Heavy. Heavy and smooth inside. I don't feel where my old skin was. Or is. I get cold. If it's not hot I freeze."

"Doesn't it hurt?"

"Not if I take this." She reached into her case, took out a phial of milky liquid and held it up to the light.

"What is it?"

She shrugged. "Hunt's potion."

"And what's in it?"

"I've no idea, but it keeps me stable."

"And when you fail to take it?"

She shook her head and showed me a syringe. "It feels like my real skin's crawling to get out, as if I'm on fire. You've heard me."

"So why were you in Somerset?"

"He needed isolation. Once he'd made the skin grow, he decided it was best to get out of Cambridge. That house, the one you came to, used to belong to his mother. I think she left it to him…"

"Once he had got it to grow?"

"Yes. Then he had to keep me alive."

I shook my head.

"What are you thinking?" she said.

"I don't know."

"You don't know what?"

"It's mad."

"Apart from Hunt, you're the only person who's seen me."

"Seen you?"

"Since it happened."

"So why didn't he show you to his colleagues? If he wanted to prove his ideas…"

She shrugged and said, "I don't know. Maybe he thought they'd be horrified, or the authorities would take him in." She stared at me and her eyes dilated. "Are you?"

"Am I what?"

"Horrified?"

"Yes."

"Yes."

"At what he has done to you… it is…"

"But me? What I look like…"

"I'm looking at you, but I don't think I am. I have to fool myself into thinking that I'm seeing you like you were before, and I'm doing that because otherwise I'd go mad."

"That's it," she said, "precisely. It's how I've learnt to think. When I see myself in a mirror, I have to force myself to remember how I used to be, how my skin was. How smooth and pink it was. But I suppose... I suppose that's over. Now... now I'm this."

"And what was going to happen to you? If I hadn't met you, if you'd stayed in Somerset, what was he going to do with you?"

"I'm not sure. Some experiments fail, others succeed. Maybe I'd have become his stolen masterpiece."

"I'm sorry?"

"You know, the stolen painting that's so famous the new owner doesn't dare show it to anyone. But it doesn't matter anyway, because the pleasure's in the owning, the keeping, never the display. Maybe I was all about possession. Possession and proof."

"Proof?"

"That his theories were possible."

"Mad," I said.

"Oh yes," she said, "quite mad. But careful with it."

I went to the window, looked at the back of the houses and the trees in the gardens, and I watched a jay clicking and chattering through the branches. It was trying to scare a blackbird, but the blackbird was brave and would not fly away. It sang its song as though its heart would burst. I took a bottle of sherry down and said, "Can you drink?"

"I have no idea."

"Do you want to?"

"Yes," she said, "I think I do."

I fetched a couple of glasses, poured, drank, watched her sip and asked about her parents.

"I have written to them, once. It was difficult, but I didn't want them to worry. My mother especially – she's a great worrier."

"What did you tell them?"

"I said I was in Scotland, working on an important experiment I couldn't say anything about."

"Do you want to write now?"

"Tomorrow," she said. "When I'm ready."

"We might not have time," I said.

"Why not?"

"Because someone else did see you."

"Who?"

"Miss Watson."

"Who's Miss Watson?"

"At Belmont. The house I was working in. She saw us leave. The first thing Hunt will do is ask her where I live. And if she doesn't tell him, someone will. Maybe the solicitor..."

"What solicitor?"

"Mr Prior-Stewart. He visited Miss Watson about Belmont."

Isabel held up her glass and said, "This feels very nice."

"Good." I swilled my own glass, drank, swallowed and said, "We could call the authorities."

"The authorities?" Now she laughed. "What good would that do?"

"I don't know, but we could get him locked up."

She shrugged. "Call them if you want, but I won't talk to them."

"Why not?"

"Because…" she said, and she ran her hands up her arms across her shoulders and over her chest, "because I'd be taken away." She sat back and finished her drink, closed her eyes and made a rattling sound in her throat. "And I don't want that." She looked around the kitchen. "I want this…"

"So…"

"So?"

"So we spend tonight here, but we'll have to leave tomorrow. I'm owed some time. I have to visit the office for an hour, but then we'll go."

"Go where?"

"I know a place."

"Where?"

"You'll see."

"And what will happen then?" Her voice went up. "What will happen to me?"

"Isabel… I don't know," I said, but then I could not say any more, and poured myself another glass of sherry.

When it was dark she went to the window and said she wanted to go outside. We were half drunk. I looked at her and tried to see her as she should have been, with human skin and curly brown hair and nice clothes. She slurred her

words, flapped her arms and said I reminded her of someone
she knew in Cambridge. It was my nose and something to
do with the way I talked. Or my eyes.

"You want to go for a walk?" I said.

"Yes."

"But people will see you."

"I don't care."

"I think you do."

"I…" she jabbed a finger at me, "do not."

"Then we go out."

"We go out…"

"And what do you want to do?"

"Let's see." She finished her drink, got up, staggered
and steadied herself against the wall. She reached for her
coat, pulled it on, and asked if she could borrow a scarf.
I found one; she wrapped it around her face so only her
eyes were showing, pulled the cowl up and said, "What
do you think?"

"You look mysterious."

"I am," she said, "infinitely. And now I'm going to take the
night air." And she was out of the door before I had time to
grab my wallet.

I ran to catch up with her and joined her on the pavement.
We crossed the road to the Fields, and then she shouted and
dashed away, running from tree to tree. "Yes!" she yelled, and
when I caught up with her she said, "Do you remember the
first time you saw me?"

"How could I forget?"

"Never forget!" she said, and she ran off again.

When I caught up with her, she jumped from behind a tree, grabbed my hand and, as we headed towards Upper Street, she said, "Where are we?"

"Highbury."

"I think I like Highbury."

"So do I. Have you been here before?"

"No. But Hunt has a house in Kew. Is that close?"

"No."

"I was there for a night before we moved to Somerset. You can see the palm house from the top floor. Do you know the palm house?"

"Yes," I said, and before I could tell her about the hours I had spent in Kew Gardens, she ran away from me again and hid behind another tree.

She jumped out again, laughed and said, "You don't know how much you miss people until you can't see them any more. Strangers... strangers and lights. Street lights, shop lights, the traffic," and as we crossed the road she was suddenly transfixed by an omnibus. I had to pull her out of the way as the driver yelled, "Dozy cow!" – and as she laughed back, the scarf slipped from her face. The driver saw her scales and his face went white before we were back on the pavement. I stopped her in a doorway and said, "Are you sure this is a good idea?"

"Of course it is. Why shouldn't it be?"

I reached up, adjusted her scarf and said, "No reason. No reason at all," and we walked on, my arm around her shoulders and her head tight against me. When we passed a public house, she stopped and said, "I want to go inside."

"Not tonight. They're closing."

"But I want to." She looked at me and said, "Just for a moment. I want to remember what it was like. It's been so long. Please?"

Her eyes pleaded, and it was impossible to refuse her, so I opened the door and guided her through the saloon bar to the snug. There I found a corner table, and while she settled herself, I went to order our drinks.

I fetched a pint of mild for myself and a glass of sherry for her, placed them on the table and sat beside her. We chinked our glasses, sipped, and she moved as close to me as she could and whispered in my ear, "Do I scare you? Do I make your skin crawl?"

"No."

"Did I ever?"

"When I first saw you I think I was more amazed than anything else. Maybe a little scared."

"I never meant to."

"I want to see beyond it," I said.

"Why?"

"Because I think..."

"Because you think what?"

"I'm not sure," I said, though maybe even then, even though I had only known her for two days, I was.

* * *

The beer was not the best, but it did its work, and as we drank, the conversation turned to sweethearts. She said she could not understand why I did not have one, and I mumbled something about someone I met in Edinburgh, and how it had failed for no discernible reason.

"What do you mean?"

I felt myself redden. "You must know," I said, "how it is."

"No," she said. "Explain. What was her name?"

"Grace," I said, and as I pronounced the name, I felt a well open in my body, and all my emotions began to trickle over its edge and tumble down. I shook my head. "I'll tell you all about her one day, when we know each other better."

"You promise?"

"I promise," I said, and I picked up my glass and stared into my drink and thought about Edinburgh and how, maybe, things could have been different.

Listen, I call through time, Grace. Grace. Can you hear me? Are you there? Could things have been different? Could you have changed the course of my life? Could you have taken my reservations and imaginings and turned them to the good? And where are you now? What has happened to you? Are you happy with a gentleman you met at a tea dance or as you walked along a windy strand? I hate asking or writing questions, though I have to and I do care, care more than you ever knew I could.

I have these pictures.

I have them framed.

Look.

I can say I met her in my last year at Edinburgh. She worked in the university library, and although I thought her lovely eyes and soft hair and whispered words were sent from heaven to be with me, I did not act upon my feelings for at least – I would say – a few months. But one evening I was working too hard at my books, and she was obliged to ask me to leave the library as she was locking up the building.

"Locking up?" I said.

"Yes," she said. "I'm sorry. I have to." She touched her cheek.

"Could you give me another five minutes?"

"I'm sorry," she said. "I have my orders." And she looked over her shoulder towards the head librarian, a severe man with no hair and stains and crumbs on his jacket who stood by the main door and scowled at me.

"Oh well," I said – I think I said – and I closed my books, stacked them under my arm and, as she disappeared to I do not know where, left the library.

Half an hour later, I called into a tea shop for some early-evening refreshment, and as I sat down, noticed her at the far end of the shop. She was alone, eating a small cake. I went over to say hello: she said she was waiting for a friend, and when I asked her if I could join her for a few minutes, she gestured at the empty chair, nodded, said "Please do", and we shared a pot of Darjeeling.

I asked her about the library, and as she talked about books, the tottering stacks and her work, I thought she had the most beautiful smile I had ever seen. I resolved to tell her, but lost my nerve. In those days, women and lost nerves walked hand in hand in my mind. They would look into each other's eyes and smile, nod a nod of mutual understanding and move quickly on to something else. They were like the words I tried to put together – dropped, failed. I asked her about other things: her family, what books she had read and music. She said she loved Palestrina and Chaucer. I liked the way she spoke. She had a light voice and never put a word out of place, stringing them into her sentences like a jeweller would thread gems on a string. And there was something familiar about her eyes. Had I seen them in a picture? In a reflected window on a grey street? And when she touched her hair and flicked some strands away from her eyes, I felt the first twinge of an unfamiliar feeling.

I think she felt it too, but before we had the chance to act on our feelings, her friend arrived and I gave up my seat, saying, "I hope we'll meet again."

"I'm sure we will," she said, and gave another smile.

We met the next day at the library, and the next, and the next, and met for tea, and the following week we visited the National Gallery to look at the paintings. Another week passed, and another, and one Tuesday we attended a performance of Pierre de la Rue's Missa Sancta Dei Genetrix and afterwards, as we walked across The Meadows, she turned to me, blinked her beautiful eyes and said, "Are we courting?"

"Yes," I said, "I think we should be," and so it was. She smiled, said, "Then I think I might take your arm," and she did as we walked, and I think I heard a flute somewhere, or the echo of indecision crashing onto a lonely beach somewhere, losing itself for ever.

A month later, I travelled to Leith to meet her mother and father. She was a quiet woman who spoke – if I remember well – no more than a dozen words, but baked – and I do remember this well – a perfect fruit cake. He was a prosperous man, a Presbyterian corn merchant, proud of his only daughter, and anxious that any man who showed an interest in her came from a good, God-fearing family. I think he was pleased my father was a man of God, though something about the liberality of the Church of England rankled. He asked me a few questions about faith, and although I did not betray my true feelings, I did not lie. So when he smiled and shook my hand and said, "I trust your intentions are honourable," I said, "Naturally, Mr Jackson." And with that – I assumed – a blessing was bestowed.

How did our lives develop? For six months, we spent every free moment together, and she showed me places I might never have seen without her. We walked the windy crags of Arthur's Seat, explored the Closes of the Old Town, and – my favourite – the hidden secrets of the Botanic Gardens. One weekend we even travelled to the far north-west to her cousin's house near Sandwood Bay, and as we walked along the shore, I felt myself falling in love, and I think she felt the same. We even expressed our desire in ways that would have shocked our parents, and as our relationship started to take the inevitable steps towards the moment when I would stand before her father and ask his permission, we talked about the future in serious, religious terms. Where would we live? What direction would my career take? What about hers? What sort of home would we choose? And would we have two children, or four?

She had strong opinions about many things – art, literature, politics – and I put up with her occasional rants. In return she put up with my silences – my broods, she called them – and as the months passed, we settled into regular patterns, regular walks, regular conversations. In the end we agreed that Edinburgh would be a fine place to live, floral wallpaper would be perfect for a hallway, and the more window boxes the better. We started to look at rings in jewellery shops, but then, shockingly and for no apparent reason, the relationship cooled, like the day you know summer's changed to autumn. It happened overnight, a chill wind, leaves that were not a pleasure to kick through, an overcast sky. And although we both asked each other what the trouble was, neither of us could understand the change, and before we knew it we were not seeing each other every day. Then we missed a weekend together, and when we tried to talk about plans, the plans had faded. One day she told me that she wanted some time alone – "How long?" "I don't know." "Why?" "I don't know." – and by the end of the year the relationship was over. There were no third parties, just cold winds. The separation was not acrimonious, and when we said goodbye for the last time we were both weeping, but there was no going back, no going forward and nowhere else to go. And as I settled back into a single life and avoided the university library, I began to wonder if the feelings other people described as love were either lies or feelings I would never understand or enjoy. It was impossible for me to tell, and at that time, as I nursed my wounds and thought my heart hurt, I did not bother to ask myself important questions. Maybe I lacked the capacity for big emotions. I do not know. Maybe my mother's death had robbed me of something. Maybe, without thinking, my father had planted the seed of detachment in my head and it grew without my knowing. Or maybe I am leading blame out of its stable, taking it down to a stream and letting it whinny and drink. It is far too easy to do this sort of thing, as though blame really is a horse and all our campaigns depend on it.

I would have loved to have taken Grace to Norfolk. We could have visited in the spring when the marshes are teeming with nesting birds and the sky bleeds its clearest light. We could have healed the wounds, but we did not. I remember thinking we could have had a perfect time there, and I thought about the perfect times we had in other places and how I looked for her for months after we parted. I did. I was more upset than I thought I would be, and even now I catch my breath when I see a particular hairstyle – straight and soft with a side parting, cut off the neck, full at the back – and a particular type of mouth. Grace had sweet lips, a cluster of beautiful birthmarks on her face and knew more about

Chaucer than anyone I ever met. When I think about our time together, I think it was too fine, but maybe the lack of drama and power were the things that brought the relationship to an end. And then I think there was love there, but maybe I never believed it and thought it was bound to fail. Maybe I forced this, like a fool. Self-fulfilling prophecies are easy to believe, and when you doubt its existence, love is too difficult to hold.

Isabel and I sat in silence for a few minutes until she suddenly said she wanted to go on holiday. She wanted to sit by a blue sea or walk over grass-topped cliffs where people could fly kites or lie behind hedges, and sometimes she wanted this so much she ached. She talked about Charmouth, and I told her I had been at school in Dorset. A faraway look came into her eyes, and I said we could go back. We could visit some places I knew and see her parents, but she said, "I can't. Not until..."

"Until what?"

"Until... you know." She rubbed the back of her hand.

"I know somewhere else we could go."

"Do you?"

"Yes," I said. "It's safe, in Norfolk."

"Norfolk? I like Norfolk. Is it by the sea?"

"Yes. In the marshes. Hidden..."

"It sounds lovely."

"It is," I said, and as she nodded and lowered her scarf to take a sip of her sherry, I said, "When he did this... what happened?"

"What do you mean?"

"You know… how did he do it?"

She squinted at the memory. "I'd been with him for a couple of months. We'd been working well, and I suppose – I don't know – maybe we were becoming more than simply colleagues. Not that we ever did anything improper, but every now and again he'd look at me in an odd way."

"What sort of odd way?"

"An 'odd' odd way."

I nodded.

"And then one day he told me about these ideas he'd been working on. I didn't believe what he was talking about. Fooling cells? He said he'd had some success with mice but could only prove his theories if he had a human to work with. Would I be interested? He told me there'd be more money for me if I agreed, and I might need a few days' rest, but I'd be up and around in no time at all. A few days' rest…" She sipped her sherry.

"So about six months ago, he started me on a course. Intravenous injections of some potion he'd developed. At first nothing happened, and he began to think he'd failed. That was a bad time. He's got a short temper and he blamed me. I didn't have the right biological make-up, and when I told him there was nothing wrong with my biological make-up, so why didn't he use himself as a guinea pig, he told me that there were hundreds of people who'd give their right arm to work with him.

"But then it started. I had no warning. At first, I thought I had a rash, but I knew. They were scales. They appeared on my stomach, and when I went to bed there was a cluster about this size." She made a circle with her finger and thumb. "In the morning, they were the size of a plate, and half my hair had fallen out. I thought I was going mad. When he saw me, he was silent for a while, and then he started grinning. A mad, wild grin, and it didn't take me long…"

"To what?"

"To ask the question."

"What question?"

"Why was I so stupid?"

"You weren't."

"I should have seen through him. I should have seen it coming. That first morning. Every time I looked at myself there were more scales. By the evening I could see them growing. He'd locked me in – all I had was a mattress and a bucket. And once I'd got past the thought that I wasn't dreaming, that this was real, all I could think about was trying to kill myself. That was something I'd never thought about before. Never. Kill myself? I love living. Loved…"

I had nothing to say, so I drank.

"About twenty-four hours after it started I was almost completely covered in scales. Now he was very happy. He gave me a sleeping draught, and when I woke up we were in that place."

"Ashbrittle?"

"Yes."

"And during that time?"

"It was hell. I had weeks of despair. I was scared of myself. What do people say about being scared of your own shadow? I'd look at my reflection in a window and scream. I slept all day and half the night. I couldn't stand up for longer than five minutes without nodding off. My concentration went and the potion he dosed me with made me bleed pus." She looked at her glass and pushed it away.

"But one day he got the dose right and I began to feel better. Better inside, anyway. I'd still look at myself and want to throw up, but then I thought…"

"What did you think?"

"I thought I'd beat him. I was still tired, but I promised myself I'd escape. I tried a couple of times, but never got further than the door. The door…" she said and she suddenly dropped her head. She took a deep heaving breath, but it sounded like the air would not go down. She rattled and gasped and gripped the table.

"Isabel?"

She shook her head, held her stomach and retched.

"Are you sick?"

"I can't…" She took another huge breath.

"Isabel?"

"Can't…"

"Isabel?"

"Aaah…" she gasped again, then stopped and doubled up.

"What's the matter?"

She retched again, gulped and hissed, "I..."

"What?"

"I..."

I reached across the table and touched her arm. She pulled it away.

"Help..."

"Isabel..."

"Help me..."

"What do you need?"

"I need..." She gasped. "Need..."

"Yes?"

"Need to get out..."

"What is it?"

"I need my stuff..." she said and she doubled up again. Her head slumped forward and banged on the table. A couple of people looked towards us, but the place was busy and we were just another couple who might have had too much to drink. I put my arm around her shoulders, covered her face with the scarf, slapped the hat on her head and guided her through the crowds, out of the snug and into the street.

As soon as we were outside, she started to panic and shake, and her hands flapped like wings in front of her face. I put my arms around her and helped her down the road, and although she managed to contain herself, by the time we reached Highbury Corner she was trembling, whimpering and rubbing her arms. People were staring at us and giving us plenty of room, and when we were across the road and onto the Fields I said, "Almost there." She looked up, broke away and ran through the trees. I lost her behind them and saw her again as she dashed back across the road and through the gate to my building.

She was sitting on her haunches, sobbing and slapping her knees. The light from the gas lamps was fanning through the bushes that surrounded the front door. She had taken the hat off, and the scales that covered her head and ran down her back were winking. I opened the door, put my hands under her arms, picked her up and carried her the two flights to my rooms.

She weighed nothing. I could feel her bones through her clothes and her breath against my cheek. It was hot and smelt of eggs and sherry. I sat her on the floor outside my door, picked her up again, stumbled over the mat, slammed my knee against the hall table, laid her on the settle, fetched the bag from the kitchen and knelt down beside her.

"Phial," she said, "and I need a syringe."

I put one of the phials on the floor and took out a syringe. It was big and cold and bright, and the needle was long. I said, "You want me to fill it?"

"I can't."

"How much?"

"Up to twenty-five."

"I haven't done this before," I said, and as I did, her legs stiffened and foam started to bubble from her mouth. Her eyes rolled back, the muscles in her neck bulged and then she screamed. I had heard her scream before, but never so close, and never like this. For a moment I thought it was going to burst my ears and pop my eyes, and as it carried on and would not stop I waited for her head to explode and the neighbours to start banging on the door. "Be calm," I said, and as she stopped to take a breath I pushed the needle into the phial. The stuff inside smelt of the sickly-sweet smell of Hunt's house in Somerset, and as it rushed into the syringe I said, "It's coming…"

She screamed again. The pictures on my walls shook.

Twenty-five. I held it up to the light.

"Tap the air out…"

I tapped the syringe.

"Tap!"

I tapped it again.

"There." She pulled up her coat and dress and pointed at her thigh. "Here…"

I tapped the syringe again, and when she was still, I rubbed a spot on her thigh, about halfway between her waist and her knee. "Here?"

She nodded, and I found a place between two scales. I looked at the spot and touched it. The scales there were like little flattened brown seeds. They shone when I rubbed them. I looked up at her face. It was glistening with tears, and as she opened her mouth and threw her head back, foam flew away and sprayed across the carpet. I pushed the needle against her.

It took a moment's pressure to break the skin, but then it was in. I pushed the plunger, and as the liquid disappeared the scream faded to a sigh, her head dropped and she began to relax. It took a minute, but then her arms went limp, her legs next and then the rest of her body. Her breathing began to slow to normal and she let out a series of long whimpering cries. Her eyes closed and her head tipped away; she gasped and then made a long, whistling sound. Gently, down and down and she was still.

I sat beside her and stroked her hand. I whispered the first foolish words that came into my head, something like "Easy, easy..." and a couple of minutes later she opened her eyes, wiped the tears from her face and the spit from her mouth and pushed herself up. I said, "Hello..."

"David."

"Do you feel better?"

"Better?" she said.

"That's the wrong question. Sorry."

She smiled. "No. It's a normal question. I'm not used to normal questions. I haven't been asked many lately." She took a deep, wheezing breath. "And I haven't asked any."

I fetched some water. "Then may I ask you an unusual question?"

"Yes?"

"How often do you need an injection?"

"I don't know. This isn't stable." She rubbed her arms. "Sometimes I don't need any for a day, then I need it every hour. I should have taken a loaded syringe."

"And what's going to happen when this stuff runs out?"

"I don't know. There's enough for a week or two. Maybe three."

"So in a week or two you're going to have one of those attacks and you won't have anything to take for it?"

"Yes."

"And you can live with that?"

"Do I have a choice?"

"I don't know. Do you know what it's made from?"

"No."

"I think…" I could feel my heart bursting in my chest. She was looking up at me. Her head was tipped to one side and again I saw her face as it should have been, and her eyes reflected me.

"What!" she said.

"I think we should find out what it is… how it works…"

"Do you know someone?"

"I might do. A friend from university. William. He's a medical man."

"Then ask him," she said, like she did not care and wanted to do something else.

"I'll see him tomorrow."

"Do that," she said, and then, "I think I'm going to bed."

"I'll help you."

"Thank you," she said, and I picked her up, carried her to my bedroom and laid her down. I pulled the blankets over her and laid her coat over them, and sat beside her for ten minutes. I watched her and she looked at me, and then she turned away from me and her breathing slowed and I closed my eyes and watched the spots behind my lids. There were hundreds, and I let them swarm and gather, swarm away again and fly to the corners of the dark.

I was lying on the settle when I heard Isabel calling my name. I got up and went to the bedroom. She had lit a candle. The blankets were pulled up to her chin and she was wearing a woollen hat. She said, "Would you read me a story? No one's read to me for so long."

I shook my head and smiled at her. She pulled the blankets tighter and snuggled down. "Which one?"

"I don't know. They're your books. You choose."

"What do you like?"

She shrugged.

"I'll choose," I said, and I went to the shelves and ran my fingers along the spines until I found one of my favourite books. I held it to my nose. It was worn, but interesting and full of the greatest stories. I said, "How about a fairy tale?"

"Yes please," she said, so she moved to one side of the bed and I lay down on the side I do not usually sleep on. I leafed through the book and chose 'The Hut in the Forest', and when she was ready I started to read.

The story was about a poor wood-cutter who lived with his wife and three daughters in a little hut on the edge of a dark and lonely forest. Two of the daughters were lazy and badly behaved, while one was a good girl and kind to animals. I read, turned the pages quietly and, when she moved towards me, I shifted my shoulder and let her rest her head on my chest. She made little pleased sounds when good things happened to the characters, and shuddered when things went wrong. And when I reached the moral and the end, she snuggled up to me, kissed my cheek and smiled. "Thank you," she said. "That was perfect."

I closed the book, put it on the bedside table and said, "My mother used to read these to me."

"Where does she live?"

"She died," I said.

"Oh. I'm sorry."

"It was a long time ago," I said, and I told her what I knew about the accident and the rose bed and my father. As I talked, she put her hand on my chest while I ran my finger in circles around one of the patches of brown on her shoulder, and her eyes closed. After about ten minutes I felt her go limp and she made a little clicking sound that came from deep in her throat. Then, when I was sure she was asleep, I slipped off the bed, blew out the candle, left the door half open, went to the sitting room and lay back on the settle. I closed my eyes and saw forests and huts and birds, little grey men in hats, stolen cows and old horses and then, in a blinding flash of relief, sleep.

When Isabel awoke in the morning, she was sluggish and said she wanted to be left alone with the curtains drawn. I told her I was going to my office. Then I would be visiting William, and I wanted to take some of her medicine to show him. She gave me one of the phials, told me to be careful with it and, after I had given her a glass of water and a slice of toasted bread, I told her not to open the door to anyone.

When I left the building, I stood on the step for a moment. I looked for loitering people or carriages with steamed windows. Apart from a pair of tramps sitting on a bench and a clutch of ragged children baiting a dog, I saw no one who looked as though they should not be there. I walked to Highbury Corner, caught the omnibus and rode into town.

My superior was Mr Hick. He was a tall and elegant man. He always kept a carefully folded handkerchief in his top pocket and smelt faintly of cologne. He wore half-glasses, beautiful suits, and on this day a silk tie with flowers entwined. His office was tall and panelled with oak. There were a series of hand-tinted botanical prints on the walls, and a pair of Germanic vases on a low sideboard. He sat behind a huge desk and twirled a silver fountain pen. I sat in a leather wing-back, and as he skimmed my report of the Buff-Orpington collection, I gave him a précis of the highlights. He smiled, his cheeks glowed and he said, "This is wonderful, David. Wonderful. You have done very well. Quite excellent work. I'm proud of you."

"Thank you, sir."

"The Dresden Œuvres – are they really as good as you say?"

"Every bit. They're superb."

"I can't wait to see them."

Mr Hick reached across his desk and pulled out a sheaf of notes, but before he had a chance to tell me what he wanted me to do next, I said, "I'm owed some days."

He took off his glasses, squinted at me and put them on again. "Are you indeed?"

"Yes, sir."

"I see."

"And I was wondering if I could take them now, sir."

"But we wanted you in Derby in a few days. I believe you were informed. It's an important sale. We need you there, David."

"Can I see the catalogue?"

He pulled it out of the sheaf, passed it across the desk and said, "I think you might be interested."

The lots were varied, but the highlight was the Milton. There was a copy of the 1644 edition of *Areopagitica* with two corrections in the poet's own hand, *Paradise Lost* with *Paradise Regain'd* and *Samson Agonistes* all bound in one volume (1669–71), and a rare copy of the first collected edition of the great man's poetry. There were other lots of lesser editions and pamphlets, and as I leafed through the catalogue, Mr Hick said "Milton?" knowing I could not resist.

"I can see, sir."

"There are some fine editions, so naturally we thought..."

"Of course," I said, and I recalled why.

When I left university, I moved back to Dover. For a couple of weeks I walked the cliffs, read books in the freezing parlour and listened to my father as he repeated the same stories over and over again. A feeling of melancholy and lassitude began to descend upon me, but one day, a bold autumn day with golden light and a desperate wind that blew off the sea, I decided to look for a job. I wanted to work with books – that much I knew – so I wrote to publishers, antiquarian booksellers, auction houses and libraries, anyone or anywhere that would bring me into constant contact with words and pages. On a cold day in November – a Wednesday, I think – I was offered a junior position at Mitchell's, a small but respected auction house, and a job as manuscript assistant at the British Library. I chose Mitchell's, and moved to London in the first week of the coldest December for forty years.

For the first year I was assistant to a senior valuer. I loved the work, the accumulation of knowledge and the idea that I might stumble on forgotten treasure. Something overlooked, something lost, a scribbled hand on a yellowed flyleaf, a signature leaping out, but only at someone who knows what they are looking for.

Within a few months I had become so involved in the job I could not walk by a second-hand bookshop without checking its shelves, and my idea of a relaxing holiday was a week browsing the shops of Bloomsbury. And so it was that I found myself in a little place behind the British Museum, leafing through a badly chipped copy of *Tetrachordon*. I was about to put it back on the shelf when I noticed something odd about the backboard and its marbled paste-down. It was bulging, and there was a repaired cut along the top edge. I closed the book, took it to the counter and paid the asking price. I carried it back to my rooms and carefully reopened the cut with my razor. I tipped the book upside down, tapped it with the palm of my hand and a plain brown envelope dropped out.

My heart jumped. The book trade is rife with stories of amazing finds in quotidian circumstances, and as I opened the envelope the hairs on my neck froze. I was holding a short autographed letter from John Milton to an un-named lawyer. The poet thanks the man for his interest in *Areopagitica* and writes, "My belief is absolute, for books are truly as lively as the dragon's teeth I wrote of," and as I read and the paper crinkled in my hands, I could not stifle a yell. And when I look at that letter now I still bless my luck. It has become my talisman, a signpost to the future, and was the reason I dispelled any doubts about the wisdom of my choice of profession, and why I used to be a book valuer.

So when I said to Mr Hick, "I'd love to go, I really would, but why don't you send Mr Reynolds? He'll enjoy Derby," I had a catch in my voice.

"Mr Reynolds?"

"Yes sir. He's a good man."

"But does he know his Milton?"

"As well as I do."

Mr Hick took the catalogue back and flicked through the pages. "I suppose we could," he said. He looked at me. "I have to say, you do look tired."

"I'm exhausted."

"Just exhausted, David? Nothing more? I must say, I do detect a certain, how can I put it, lethargy in your manner…" Mr Hick had always taken an avuncular interest in me, and his concern was genuine.

"I just need a few days' rest, sir."

"Simply a few days?"

"Yes, sir."

He paused, flipped some pages in his diary, scribbled a note and said, "Then we'll send Reynolds." And as I left his office he said, "Going anywhere pleasant?"

"I don't know."

"Norfolk?"

"I'm not sure…"

"Well, wherever you go, do have a relaxing time," he said, and with a wave of his hand he returned to his work. I left the office, and as I stood in the hushed corridor, for a single, preternatural moment I thought that I would never see him again, never see my office again, or the beautiful view of the busy Thames, the barges and lighters and tugs, and the desperate glow on the inky water. But these were simple, foolish thoughts. I chased them away like a dog or cat, and when I reached the street I turned for a moment, looked up at the building and knew the place would always be a home to me.

* * *

I took a cabriolet to Smithfield and called on my medical friend William. His office was on the first floor of a building behind St Bartholomew's hospital. He had not changed. He was serious and studious, with thinning hair and neat, plain clothes, exactly as I remembered him. He had a nervous tic – he rubbed the side of his nose every couple of minutes – and before he answered a question he screwed up his eyes and thought carefully. I offered to buy him a cup of tea, so we left the hospital and crossed the road to a restaurant in the shadow of the meat market. It was hot, steamy and noisy, and bloodied porters came and went. We sat in a corner, sipped our drinks and for five minutes shared the awkward memories of two people who could have been best friends but drifted apart before the crucial connections were made. I say best friends but maybe not – I have no idea what I mean. What I mean is not necessarily what I say, but we talked about Edinburgh and about how our expectations had almost met our ambitions, and I asked him exactly what he was doing now.

"Laboratory work, mostly. Sometimes I get to do something interesting, but mostly it's routine."

"Do you want to do something different? Something unusual?"

"What do you mean?"

I took the phial out of my case and put it on the table between us.

"And what is this?" he said. He picked up the phial and shook it. It clouded. He squinted at it, and I could see he was intrigued.

"I have no idea, but I don't think it's anything routine."

"No?"

"A friend of mine takes it, she won't tell me what it is, and I'd like to know."

"She's addicted?"

"No."

"Then what?"

"She's sick," I said.

"And this is a prescribed medicine?"

"Not exactly."

"And what does that mean?"

I shook my head. "It's difficult to explain."

"Try."

"I can't."

"And what do you want me to do with it?"

"Could you analyse it? I'll pay you."

Now he laughed. "Nothing routine…"

"I don't think so."

He sipped his tea, put the phial on the table between us, sat back, thought for a long minute and then said, "If I do this, you don't have to pay me, but you will make a donation to the hospital."

"Of course," I said.

"Good," he said, "then I'll see what I can do," and that is how we left it, him tapping the phial and holding it up to the light, and promising to call on me in a few days.

* * *

I was going to go straight home, but as I was close to where my old friend Timothy lived, I made a visit. When he answered the door, he was wearing a dressing gown over his pyjamas and his hair looked as though it had not been brushed for a week. I followed him up to his rooms, which were littered with empty beer bottles, unwashed dishes and overflowing ashtrays. I did not bother to ask how he was, and for a moment I thought about turning around and leaving, but when he started weeping, I put a kettle on the stove and some leaves in the pot, and lit him a cigarette.

He took it with a shaking hand and said, "I'm so tired…"

"What's the trouble?"

He shook his head, took a deep drag and said, "I'm not going to spend the rest of my life working in the law."

"So what are you going to do?"

He shrugged. "I'm writing the novel. Again." He pointed at a sheaf of papers on the table. They were covered in scrawled notes and corrections.

"What's it called?"

"Well, it used to be *The Sleepwalker*, but I'm not sure any more. Maybe I'll call it *When You Hate.*"

"What's it about?"

"Parents," he said, and when I asked him why, he told me what I had suspected, that after his time in hospital he had reformed himself in response to an offer from his father: get a first and a respectable job, and I will buy you your own rooms.

"So what did he say when you told him about the novel?"

"I haven't told him."

"And when you do?"

"He'll be angry. And when he gets angry, it's best to be in the next parish."

I poured the tea, and as we drank and he smoked another cigarette, I waited for him to ask if he could move in with me, but he did not. He started to talk about writing and how he surprised himself. I asked if I could look at the work, but he shook his head and told me he could not show me anything, not yet, he was superstitious, he did not know if he was heading in the right direction anyway, he needed more time, but yes, eventually I would have the chance to read it. And when he asked me how Somerset had been I told him it was a quiet place, the Buff-Orpington collection was superb, and one day I would tell him a story he would never believe.

"What do you mean?"

"I can't tell you now."

"Why not?"

"Because..." I said, but by now he was ready to see the back of me and return to his work, so I left him sitting at the table with a distant look in his eyes and a drift of cigarette smoke settling around his head.

When I returned to my rooms, Isabel was lying in bed, wrapped in blankets and an eiderdown. The curtains were closed and the fire was dying. For a moment I thought I had stepped into the wrong rooms or an alternative version of my own rooms carried from someone else's imagination and put in place without sound or reason. I said "Hello," and she looked at me, punched the pillow and said, "My head hurts."

I sat next to her. "I'm sorry."

"And my hands. And my stomach, and my legs."

"Do you want to go?"

"Where?"

"Norfolk."

She shook her head. "What good's it going to do?"

"I don't know. But it is beautiful there. Peaceful. And you'll be safe."

"And that's going to make a difference?"

"I don't know."

"Norfolk's flat."

"Last night you said you liked the sound of it."

"I'd drunk too much sherry."

"And I drank too much beer," I said, and I got up, pulled a suitcase from under the bed, flipped it open and started filling it with clothes. I picked up a few books and tossed them in with some other things, the sort of things you might need if you are planning to leave town for a short while. Isabel sat up, ran her fingers down her arms and said, "All right, let's go to Norfolk."

I turned and faced her. The scales around her eyes were lighter than the others, and smaller, and where they covered her lids, thin and white. Our faces were inches apart, and we stared at each other for a moment until she threaded her arms around my waist, hugged me and said, "I didn't want to shout at you."

"Don't worry."

"I didn't mean it."

"I know."

"I didn't..." and she pulled away. I turned back to the suitcase and said, "I'll pack some things for you."

"Thank you," she said, and she lay back and watched me.

It was half-past three. I know this was the time because I checked it before I picked up the case and said, "I have to fetch some things from the shop. I'll be back in half an hour."

"I'll be here," she said.

I opened the door and stepped onto the landing outside my rooms. Sun was streaming in the window. It pooled on the floor, dripped over the banisters and trickled down the stairs towards the rooms below. I could hear someone playing a violin. I remember it was beautiful – a slow, melancholic melody. It matched my mood. And I remember looking at my doormat and hearing a faint shuffle. I saw a shadow rearing up behind me, dark and malevolent. It was straight and then it curved towards me, but before I could turn or duck, I was hit. I have no idea what he used or how hard it fell, but he was strong. It happened in a split second, and I was shot through with heat and pain. The sunlight failed. The music twisted and I looked up, and before I blacked out I knew who was standing over me, and I heard him say, "Fool..." But then I was gone.

No dreams, no memory and no time, just black pouring down and down to nothing.

I fell down hard. I twisted my arm behind my back and clipped my head on the skirting board. I felt the wood, but by the time I hit the floor I was unconscious. Out cold and dreaming of school. Coal-tar soap, mud peeling away from old shoes, scratching shirts, towels. The dark place under the chapel where the coal was stored. Damp towels, damp blankets, damp floors and fists.

When I was at school I avoided the worst of boy terror by being the one who sat by a window, gazed into the distance and carried a book. I only got into trouble when I opened my mouth. No one likes someone who thinks they know more than anyone else. I never thought this about myself, but there were boys who thought I did, and when I was boarding in Dorset, my chief tormentor was Nigel Russeter.

He was a promising cricketer and tipped for great things. He could bowl an unplayable ball, field like a cat, and his straight bat and superb footwork had been described by the cricket master as "a combination of the instinctive, the preternatural and the musical". This praise had gone to the boy's head, and he believed, at the age of sixteen, that he was invincible. Connections guaranteed him a place at Cambridge, where first-class cricket was also guaranteed. So when, following one of his rambling observations about the superiority of the English, I suggested to a history class that it was amazing a game as tedious as cricket was such an important element in the empire-builders' policy of divide and rule, I was smacked on the neck with a ruler by a livid Russeter, and told to look forward to a damn good thrashing.

That evening, after supper, I was walking down the top corridor, reading an atlas. I was looking at a map of Paraguay when a door opened and I was pulled into Nelson Dorm by Russeter and two of his friends, Milton St George and Perks.

Milton St George had red hair and a large face, and was always eating something, usually a piece of sponge cake. Perks was pasty and sweaty, wore glasses and sniffed a lot.

"Morris," said Russeter, as if he was surprised to see me. He had a cricket bat in his hand.

"Russeter..." I said, as if I was almost too tired to say his name.

Milton St George closed the door and stood in front of it. Perks blinked at me and licked his lips.

"So. Cricket is a tedious game?" he said. He looked at the others and they smiled.

"Yes."

Russeter shook his head. "What does your father do?"

"He's a parson."

"A parson, Morris? Not a bishop? Maybe an archbishop?"

"No, Russeter, a parson."

"And he has a nose, I hope?"

They all laughed at the joke.

"Oh yes," I said. "It's in the middle of his face."

"You see?" Russeter's face reddened and he turned to Milton St George. "He thinks he's clever."

"My father's a baron," said Milton St George.

"And mine's a judge," said Perks.

"Really," I said.

"Yes," said Russeter. "And when someone like you, someone who doesn't even deserve to be here, starts lecturing class about things he doesn't understand…"

"You tell him, Russeter," said Perks.

"Well… people like that have to be taught a lesson."

At this point, I was grabbed by Milton St George and hauled over a bed. I was pushed face down, and while Perks knelt on my shoulders and Milton St George held my legs, Russeter started hitting my backside with the cricket bat. I started to yell, and a minute later Mr Thomas the housemaster came running to see what the rumpus was about. Russeter convinced him we were all simply celebrating the end of term, and after being told that it was high time we behaved like adults, we were sent to our own dormitories to think about what we had done.

I thought carefully about what I had done, and decided to never let it happen again.

The following term, Russeter was a house monitor. And when he called me to his study and told me that my opinion of the French – I had informed a language class that they were the most cultured nation on earth – was tantamount to treason, he hit me on the head with a copy of *The Concise Oxford Dictionary*. Angry and no longer prepared to be treated like a punchbag, I grabbed a stool and pushed him in the stomach. He was surprised. I had caught him off balance, and he tipped sideways into a bookcase. The bookcase swayed, toppled over and crushed his legs. I heard a pair of nasty cracks, ran from the room and called for help. When Mr Thomas arrived, I explained that Russeter had slipped while trying to fetch a copy of *The Iliad* from the top shelf. While the matron shook her head and arranged for a doctor's visit, Mr Thomas told me I had done the right thing. And I was not to worry. My friend was strong and brave, and did I know that Hampshire County Cricket Club had offered him a place in their youth team? Boys like that, he said, were survivors.

Boys like that are not survivors. I destroyed Russeter's chances of being a cricketer, and although even he said it had been an accident, I knew he knew. He was just too ashamed to tell anyone that someone like me had beaten him, and the last I heard, he was working as a livestock auctioneer in Hampshire, dreams shattered, living in a boring town, married to a woman who grew sluggish and gave him three arrogant children.

When I woke up, I was lying on the landing. I could hear a bright, raging ringing, and beyond this, a distant piano. My downstairs neighbour was shaking me, and when I sat up he said, "What happened to you?"

I touched my head and felt the back of my neck. I had a damp, weeping bump there. It was the size of a prune. I winced. He gave me his hand and helped me up. I perched on the window sill. "I don't know," I said. The ringing got louder. My shopping basket was lying on the landing below.

"Is that yours?"

I nodded.

He fetched the basket, carried it up, put it on the floor beside me and said, "Are you going to be all right?"

"Yes," I said. "Thank you."

"Are you quite sure?"

I nodded while he poked his head into my rooms. When he looked back at me his face was white and he stammered, "Well I…" but did not finish whatever it was he was trying to say.

"Look," I said, but I could not finish what I was going to say either. He was scared and I was aching, and when I said, "Go back home. I'll be fine," he turned and went downstairs with a relieved sigh.

Isabel had put up a fight. The rug in the hall was rucked up, and the occasional table was on its side. A nice vase was smashed, and flowers and water spread across the floor. I went through to the sitting room; my old oak bookshelf was upended and books were strewn around. A candle stand my father had given me when he left Dover was lying on its side, the candles broken. The prints of Edinburgh were crooked, and an armchair was facing the wrong way. As I picked my way through the wreckage, my head heated up and the bump on the back of my neck began to throb. I kicked a cushion across the room and picked up a copy of Shakespeare's *Sonnets*. Its spine was broken. I flicked my way through the pages, lingered on the lines *"Mine eye and heart are at a mortal war, How to divide the conquest of thy sight..."* put the book on the arm of the settle and sat down. There was a whining in my ears, and my eyes watered.

For a moment I thought about calling her name, but there was no point, no point at all. I called it anyway – "Isabel?" – and as her name echoed around the rooms, I was hit by loss, as if something had been ripped out of my chest and shattered, and the pieces buried in a mine. A deep, hidden mine, a place I had visited before and thought I would never see again. I had pictures of this place and music to remind me. Sometimes I played the songs in my head while I looked at the pictures and allowed my throat to tighten. And sometimes I simply sat alone and imagined the place. I said her name again – "Isabel?" – and the sense deepened and filled, and my empty, rubbished rooms wagged their fingers at me and told me to go.

I took a hackney to Kew. It was expensive, but did I care? I did not. My head was boiling. The bruise on my neck was screaming. Sweats had broken out all over my body. My eyes were smarting. The gaps between my teeth had filled with salt and my tongue was swollen. Anger boiled inside me, and I rhymed Hunt's name over the rattle of the cab.

It was half-past four when I left Highbury and began the crawl down Upper Street. When we reached the Angel, we were forced to stop for a few minutes. There had been an accident. A child had fallen under the hooves of a horse, and a woman was wailing over the little body. I saw someone bring a blanket, as another tried to comfort the woman. There was a puddle of blood on the cobbles, and a small rag doll lay in the gutter, stained red and brown. I almost stepped out to help, but there was enough help already, and enough commotion. So I stared and listened and was taken to musing.

Ancient stones used to stand at the Angel. Thousands of years ago people came from miles to visit them, and beyond a grass oval and the high circle of stones, trees stretched towards the river, the marshes and downs. No one knows what these people did. Some say they worshipped the sun, others believe they slaughtered calves on a platform and washed the stones with the blood. The blood dried, the people left, the place looked like it had changed but it never did. Everything remains the same even though there are shops and offices and public houses there now, and the people wear smart clothes and walk their dogs on the raised pavements. Yes – I thought, wrongly as it turned out – maybe nothing really changes, and when the way was clear and we were allowed to continue our journey, all my thoughts collided in fury and crisis, and I beat my knees with my fists until we were past the King's Cross and heading towards the west.

Less than an hour later I was in Kew. I had the hackney wait for me by the entrance to the gardens, and set off to look for... what? A house? There were too many with hidden drives, and I had to stalk around walls and hedges and pretend I was lost. Dogs barked and cats arched, and once a woman asked me what I was doing and I'd better be away sharpish or she'd call her husband. She had a fat face and grey eyes. I apologized in my best voice and explained I was looking for my mother's cat. "It disappeared last week and she's frantic with worry."

"Oh, I am sorry," said the woman, different now and touching her face and hair. "I know how desperate it can be when you lose a pet. I lost my dog last year. He was such a lovely companion, such a joy," and she was about to tell me a story about love and regret and worry, but I hurried on. On and round I walked, back on myself and up dead ends, and past another two dozen houses with neat hedges and locked gates. I felt my mind as it started to thrash and fail, and was ready to turn around and go home when I came upon a house with a weedy drive and an untidy hedge. The place was big, the curtains were pulled shut and it simply shouted "This is the one!" to me. A waiting horse and carriage stood by the door. I had nothing to lose, so I went to the pair of iron gates at the end of the drive. They were open, but the drive was straight, and anyone walking up it could be seen from the house. So I walked on, climbed a low wall and jumped down into an overgrown garden. I fought my way through brambles and shrubs until I came to the edge of a lawn, and crouched behind a bush.

The place looked deserted, but there was a suitcase on the front step. I sat down and waited as I had waited in

Ashbrittle, surrounded by twittering birds and rustling voles, and I caught a smell of the countryside. I remembered hay and flies on cows and twists of wool caught in barbed wire. The sound of water running beneath the trees, stones moving through the water, one inch a day, one inch a day. I thought about yielding and I thought about chickens. I thought I heard chickens in that shrubbery in Kew, the sounds they made breaking into me, leading me to think about mad people who take other people and how change will break us all but does not have to. I picked a leaf from a bush and held its panic between my fingers, the cells in the fading leaf crying back to the bush, and all this madness kept me still and watching until the front door opened and Hunt emerged. He picked up the suitcase, lifted it onto the carriage's luggage rack, and went back to the house. I heard the door close, but it did not latch. I stood up. I listened to my body. My breathing was fast but steady. I waited a moment, then ran from the shrubbery, across the edge of the drive and up to the corner of the house.

I ducked down and walked beneath two windows to the door. I pushed it open. It made no sound and stopped halfway.

The hall was long and dark, lined with doors. There was a Chinese ginger jar on a low table, and a picture of a dog with odd eyes. They looked like grapes. At the end of the hall I could see into the kitchen, and dirty light spilt through the windows onto the floor. There was a rush mat there and dust balls in the corners.

When I was eight, my school friend Simon Harmon told me about dust balls. They waited under your bed, and when you were asleep they stole your dreams, stored them in their minds and worked out what you wanted. They had millions of eyes and could look in every direction at once, even inside themselves. They whispered to each other, and when I was at school and sunlight filled my room, they came out from under my bed, sat in groups and composed music. They sold the music to the motes that chimed in sunlight, but kept the finest tunes to themselves. Like Mozart, they believed rests were the best parts of music, but by this time I did not know what Simon was talking about. But I listened to him because his father was a surgeon and had once attended a minor member of the Royal Family who had a skin complaint.

Dust balls and motes enjoyed a symbiotic relationship. The motes returned the favour by finding dust and carrying it to the balls and building eyes out of grit. They could also build ears, mouths, tongues and fingertips, but eyes were their favourites. I think Simon Harmon became a surgeon too, but I am not sure. I remember he was a good singer, had blonde hair and believed tunnels riddled the ground beneath the streets of Dover.

I heard someone moving about upstairs, and a chair scraped across the floor. I stepped inside and stood at the bottom of the stairs. The air smelt damp and old, like the air in a church-hall kitchen. I heard him shout, "Get up!" and a door slammed. The sound of his voice sent the blood racing to my head. I did not think. I climbed the stairs without worrying about stepping on a loose board, and was halfway up when I saw Isabel. She was standing on the landing, wearing a white coat. I leapt up the last stairs as Hunt appeared behind her. His hair was wild and his face was shining with sweat. He was carrying the black bag, and the surprise of seeing me there stopped him in his tracks. For a second, he showed me his shrewd and charming face, but then the mask dropped, the darkness came and he narrowed his eyes. "You!" he hissed.

"Yes," I said to him, and then I yelled "Get down!" at Isabel. She dropped to her knees. As soon as she did I put my head down, jumped over her, ran towards him and smashed into his chest. He grabbed the door frame, swivelled and pushed me over. I rolled onto the floor, turned and looked up. As I did, he threw the bag at my head. I ducked, and as the bag hit the floor, it broke open and phials of the potion she needed spilt out. Some rolled across the landing, slipped through the banisters, dropped onto the stairs and smashed. More bumped against the skirting board as Hunt shouted something in German and aimed a kick at my head. I grabbed his foot and pulled him over, and as he fell I punched him in the stomach. The air shot from his body with a squeal, and when he was down I stood up and stamped on the small of his back. "Go!" I yelled to Isabel. She grabbed the bag, scooped up as many phials as she could and ran down the stairs.

As she disappeared, Hunt turned over and pushed himself up. His face was screwed with fury, and blood was dripping from his nose. He caught some on his tongue and spat it at me. I swivelled and kicked him in the chin. He made a sound like a hot glass shattering on a tin table. Two of his teeth fell out. He pointed at me and opened his mouth, but before he could say anything he fell back, lay on the floor and let out a long sigh.

My foot hurt, and I wanted to be sick. Bile shot into my mouth. My teeth felt like silver. More blood came from his nose and bubbled over his lips. I doubled up, and flashes of light came and ripped behind my eyes.

I looked over the banisters. Isabel was crouching in the hall, the black case tucked into the space between her knees and chin.

"David?" she said.

"Yes…" I said.

Hunt wheezed.

I stood up, wobbled and stepped on a phial. As it cracked, the sweet smell exploded around me. Isabel wailed. I heard a dog barking. There was a window at the end of the landing, and a tree outside. Its branches were rubbing against the glass. I said, "Give me the bag."

Isabel climbed the stairs. I picked up three phials. Hunt was quiet but breathing. She looked at him. She said, "Wait a minute," and opened a door. I saw an unmade bed, clothes on the floor, a desk and long, heavy curtains. She fetched a brass waste-paper bin from beneath the desk, came back and as she stepped over Hunt she slammed it against the side of his head as if it was something she had only just thought of doing. He gasped, and blood trickled from the wound. She looked at the bin in her hand like she was surprised to see it and did not understand what was going on, and threw it down the landing, turned, pushed past me and walked down the stairs. I picked up the bag and followed. She took her coat from a rack by the front door, wrapped it over the white coat and pulled the cowl over her head. She stepped outside and started to run. I caught up with her in the street, took her hand and pulled her towards the gardens.

I did not run, but we did move quickly, and when we reached the hackney, I ordered the driver to whip his horse into a sweat, for we had an appointment to keep. I did not have to repeat the instruction, and although we moved fast and faster still, I felt like a man on a slow winter railway train, leaning forward, pressing his nose against the glass, looking out at the cold and wondering how anyone can live out there, so alone and lost in dreams that have bought the wrong ticket. Lights burning in the daytime. Clothes frozen on a line, a cat picking its way along a wall. Snow. Trees, houses and a stream of fury bursting over the heads of anyone who saw us. Listening to the sounds of the tracks, watching my reflection on the glass, looking through the reflection, turning away. The smell of old food. The end of things and loneliness that drills into your heart and will not turn back. And as we crossed the river, I wished I was still a pleased book valuer with comfortable rooms and pictures on the wall. I wished I still believed in reason. I wished these things, but all my wishes crashed and the pieces scattered. I saw them spread out before me, every one drifting away in a suspension of its own solution. Isabel sat next to me and I looked ahead, looked at her, and she turned her head. It was impossible now, and there was only one thing we could do. Her scales glittered, the yellows glowed and the browns deepened, and as her eyes grew bigger than dishes they reflected mine, and I saw all my fears bound by her.

Norfolk

A few weeks after his retirement, about a year before I was asked to value the Buff-Orpington collection, I do not know how long after my mother was killed, my father invited me to his new home in Canterbury. We sat in his sitting room. He looked tired and bent, and could not concentrate on anything. The salvation of archery was to come, and the sooth of the butts and targets. The cathedral bells chimed the hour and, after drumming his fingers on the mantelpiece and sighing at the empty fireplace, he gave me a sealed envelope. It contained the deed to the little wooden house in Norfolk. It was in my name. He said he had bought the place when my mother was alive and it had been their intention to move there one day. Now he said, "I want you to try and find the happiness we never could."

"Thank you." This was barely adequate, but I said it anyway.

"I never want to see the place again."

"Why not?"

Saying "Why not?" to my father was not something he encouraged, but now, with Dover behind him and boxes of possessions in the hall, he began to relax and showed me a side to his nature I had not seen before. He told me that until my mother's death he had lived a devout and pious life, but after the accident had suffered a loss of faith that left him shocked and on the verge of serious melancholy. "We were so very close, David," he said. "Words like love are bandied about too easily, but I believe we truly loved each other. I was guilty…"

"Of what?"

"I should have sought consolation in my faith, done as I preached, but I took my grief out on the church, my parishioners…" He looked me straight in the eye, and I looked back at him, again, something he had never encouraged. "And I may have taken it out on you."

"No you didn't."

He looked at me, shook his enormous head and said, "I think I did. In fact, I know I did. I didn't understand."

I did not argue. There was no point as he sat there wearing a plain collar for the first time in decades, and I sat with the deed to the place in Norfolk resting on my lap and the sound of the river running beside the house. I stood up, went to the boxes in the hall and carried one of them upstairs, while he made a jug of lemonade and opened a packet of his favourite biscuits.

Isabel and I caught a train to Norwich, and I hired a horse and gig from a man who knew my father from the old days. It was late afternoon when we left his stables and took the road over the flat lands to the coast. I drove fast, but it was not fast enough for us. Isabel was cold, and although I had wrapped her in every blanket I could carry, she shivered as she dozed. The evening crept up on us, so by the time we reached the head of the track that leads to the place, the way was moonlit. But the horse was sure, and I could see the ruts, and when the house came into view, I pulled over, stopped the cart, and as the horse heaved, the noise of the marshes grew around us and the place rustled its beautiful sound.

"Home," I said, and we sat for five minutes, and listened and tipped our heads back.

She climbed down first, and I showed her the way through the gate, down the thin garden, over the lawn, past the bushes, the borders and the pond with the statue of a dog.

I climbed the steps to the veranda, unlocked the door and let it swing back on its hinges. The smell of oranges and dust and stale wine drifted out.

We stepped inside, and while I lit candles, she stood by the kitchen table and sniffed. She went to one of the side windows, looked out and touched the curtains. She turned and at first I thought she was going to cry, but then the twitches in her mouth turned up and she whispered, "I love this place."

"Good," I said.

"It's as beautiful as you said."

"I know," I said, and I laid the fire.

She went to the bedroom, came back, stepped outside and said, "Can I hear the sea?"

"Yes." I pointed. "It's over there."

"Where's the nearest village?"

"A couple of miles that way."

The fire started to blaze, and I hung a kettle over the flames while she sat at the table and picked at a splinter of wood.

"Are you all right?"

She carried on picking until the splinter broke off. She turned it over in her fingers, then looked in my eyes and said, "Did I kill him?"

"He was breathing when we left."

"He deserves to die."

Half of me did not want to agree, but the rest did, so I nodded and said, "Maybe he did. Maybe."

"He did."

I nodded, but there was no time to say anything else. I had to stable and water and feed the horse.

When the sun set, the sky bowled over the marshes and lit up with gashes of orange and pink. A flock of curlews flew to their roosts. A chill hit the air, but Isabel wanted to sit on the veranda. I wrapped her in blankets, carried her outside, put her in a chair, draped an eiderdown over the chair, put a scarf around her neck and a woollen hat on her head. I sat next to her. After supper she had felt sick and needed some of her potion. I injected her, she slept for an hour and then she wanted to smell the sea. She took deep breaths and rustled in the blankets.

As we settled down, a long, low boom echoed across the marshes, hung in the air and faded away. Another came, closer, and then the first again, like someone blowing across the top of a bottle. Isabel sat up, turned and said "What's that?"

"A bittern. It's a bird."

"I know what a bittern is." The second called and the first answered.

"They sound like something else."

"They're very shy."

Boom.

"What are they doing?"

"Calling to their mates."

Boom.

We listened to the sound, and as the dusk's breeze blew, the marshes began to whisper. I thought about telling her more about bitterns and how they stab rivals to death with their beaks, and each has its own call and they walk by grasping the reeds with their toes and using them as stilts because they hate getting their feet wet, but she said, "Have you got a kite?"

"No."

"That's a pity."

"Why?"

"I'd like to fly one. Do you like them?"

I nodded. "I used to fly them on the cliffs. The white cliffs of Dover. Shall I buy one?"

"Yes please," she said, so first thing in the morning, while she sat up in bed and drank tea, I rode into Sheringham. The lady in the shop remembered me from years before, asked after my father, and said she thought my house needed a coat of paint. "We were down that way last month," she said, "and I hope you don't think we were prying, but we did have a little look over the garden gate, and Henry noticed the way the wood was showing through. I know he'd be happy to do the work for you."

"Let me think about it," I said, and while she served another customer, I chose a red kite with a long tail. After another conversation about the importance of proper house maintenance, I left the shop and crossed the road to the second-hand bookshop. I could not help myself.

I scanned the shelves quickly and was disappointed. I found a worn two-volume encyclopedia of British birds, but most of the stock was the stock you see in every second-hand bookshop: scuffed books waiting for strangers, frightened, lonely books, lost in nothing but their own stories. And here and there a book with an unbroken spine, an unread story, the saddest thing in the world. Gasping words and wheezing sentences, vain clauses, deluded characters screaming for someone, anyone – be with me, please. Listen to me. Hear my voice. I am here. Fading in a dusty row at the edge of the country with no one but Mrs Price, the biggest gin drinker in Norfolk, for company. Biographers, novelists, poets, travel writers waiting for luck or nothing. I bought the two volumes of birds and then rode back, and when Isabel was dressed and ready we left the house and walked through the marshes.

Pure daylight changed the look of her skin. It did not seem so shiny. The yellow was paler and the browns not so deep. When we reached the beach she ran to the tide line, waited for a wave and raced it. The shingle rustled and a good breeze blew off the sea. There were a few other people walking there, so we headed towards Blakeney Point, and when we reached an empty place where the beach flattened, I asked Isabel to hold the kite while I walked away and unravelled the line. I was about to tell her to let go when the wind gusted, ripped it out of her hands and spun it into the air.

It rose quickly, and as I played the line out she ran towards me and yelled, "Let me fly it!"

I have no idea what a good kite-flyer looks like, but I think she was one. She had an instinctive feeling for what the thing was going to do next. When it started to dip, she twitched the line and pulled it back, gave out another yard and let it soar. Then she dropped her hands and it made a huge circle in the sky – the tail whizzed, she unravelled another yard and it climbed again.

"I used to fly kites!" she yelled. The wind whistled and shingle raced back with the tide. "On Stonebarrow!" Her voice ripped away and strips came down. "We used to send messages up the string!"

"Who for?"

"For the angels!"

"Did they read them?"

"Of course!" And she dropped her hands and let it whizz again, and the tail thrummed as it dived towards the beach.

"What did they say?"

"Hello!"

"Hello?"

"That's what we used to say."

"Who's we?"

"Simon and me. My brother."

"And did they send an answer?"

"Never!" she said, and she spun on her heels, dropped the line behind her back and watched the kite swoop left, right and drop and climb again.

We flew the kite for an hour. We played out all the line and, as we watched, some gulls came and dived at it for a few minutes, then lost interest and flew away. Her arms got tired easily, so we took turns, and when she had had enough she sat on the sand and watched me. I tried to do some tricks, but failed and began to reel it in. When it lost air it dropped and dived into the beach, flapped, somersaulted and died on the shingle.

I reeled in the string. She took my arm and we walked back to the house, over the dunes and through the reeds, and I propped the kite next to the front door.

"Yes..." she said.

"Yes what?" We sat on the veranda.

"This is the place."

"What do you mean?"

"This is the place..."

"Yes?"

"I can die here."

"You can what?"

"I think you heard me."

I did not raise my voice, but felt a rush of anger, pushed it back, stamped on it and kicked it into the corner. "You're not going to die, Isabel."

"I think I am. I think I will. I was thinking about it yesterday. And this is the perfect place to do it."

"What do you mean?"

"Don't be foolish, David."

"I'm not being foolish."

"It doesn't suit you. Think about it. I've got nine phials left." She pointed at the case. "Whatever happens, I'll run out by next week and then…" She took one out and held it to the light. "And then…"

I remembered the sound of two violins in a song I know, a sound of such longing and melancholy I used to hear it playing in my mind when I went to sleep, and wake up with it still playing.

"What are you thinking?"

"I think…"

"Yes?" She folded her arms and bent her head towards me.

"I think my friend William will have the answer. He'll tell me what's in those phials, and know how to make some more." I touched her face and ran my fingers over her lips.

"Professor Hunt…" she said. "He was a genius. Is William a genius?"

"I don't think so."

"No?" she said on the veranda of the house with the birds singing in the marshes and the kite flapping against the propped door.

"No."

"Then I don't think he'll have any answer at all."

We went inside, and she sat down while I stoked the fire. Then I made some tea, and while it brewed we listened to the wind and the gentle sucking of the ground, and I thought about how the reeds were like bars to our lives, keeping us safe and holding us in, and leaving us wanting nothing.

Isabel dozed, and after she had eaten an apple, she washed and went to bed. She put her head round the door and whispered, "Good night." Her skin looked flat, like land as dusk whines across the horizon and birds call. I held my arm up and said "Yes", and then sat back with a volume of my new encyclopedia. The engravings were very beautiful, but when I started to read the text, my eyes began to swim. I had started to wonder if I should buy a pair of reading glasses when she called my name. I went in to see her. She was sitting up, staring straight ahead and rubbing the scales on her arms. I said, "I thought you were asleep."

She shook her head and said, "I was thinking about what you said."

"What did I say?"

"You know."

"Do I?"

"Yes. And I was thinking about something else."

"What?"

She ran her fingers up her arms to her neck and stroked her chin. "If I wasn't like this…" Her voice trailed away.

"Yes?"

"Would you?"

"Would I what?"

"You know," she said.

"No," I said, "I don't know. Tell me."

"Would you want to walk out with me?"

I did not have to think about it. "Yes," I said, and as I said the word, she let the eiderdown slip down, looked at the patterns on her stomach and drew a figure of eight around her breasts with her fingers. "Sometimes I think I could love this skin, be proud of it. Show it to people and not care what they think. Then I think I'm mad."

"You're not mad."

"Not even a bit?"

"No."

She let the eiderdown fall to her waist. She pointed at a place on her thigh where yellow and brown scales alternated in a spiral. "This is my favourite part. I think it's like a flower."

I sat on the edge of the bed and looked at it. She took my hand and pulled it towards her leg and laid it over the spiral. I said, "Can you feel?"

She nodded, shifted to one side of the bed and said, "You can get in."

"I'm not sure."

"Why not?"

"Because... because it's not made for two people. We'll break it."

"Please..." she said.

There was nothing I could say, so I got into bed, put my arm around her and she put her head on my shoulder. When I kissed the brown oblong that crossed her forehead, tears appeared in her eyes and ran down her cheeks. She felt cold and dry, and I found a place where a couple of scales were peeling away. I licked my finger and rubbed them down.

She said, "You're a kind man."

"Sssh."

"But you are."

"I don't feel kind."

"What do you feel?"

"Difficult," I said. "I don't know. A week ago I felt fine. I was pleased with myself. Good job, nice rooms. A few friends..."

"And now?"

"Something's changed." I looked down at her. "You know that. But it's more than anything obvious, you know, because of this." I touched the scales around her eyes.

"Who are your friends?"

"There are a few people at work."

"Anyone special?"

"I've got an old friend from university. Timothy. We go drinking sometimes, but most of the time I like my own

company too much. My own company and these..." I pointed to a shelf of books.

"What's your favourite book?"

"To read?"

"What else would you do with a book?"

"In my profession there are a hundred things you can do
with a book."

"Like what?"

"You don't have to read to enjoy them. You can stare at
them. Value them. Touch them. Catalogue them. Stroke
them. If you're a barbarian, you can even tear out pages
and frame them."

"What's your favourite?"

"That depends. I love Shakespeare. You know... 'To me,
fair friend, you never can be old, For as you were when first
your eye I eyed, Such seems your beauty still.'"

"That's beautiful..."

"It is. And yours?"

"I don't have favourites."

"Favourite music?"

"It depends on the time of year."

"Place?"

"At the moment..." She narrowed her eyes. "At the
moment I'd like to go back to Charmouth. I want to
go fossiling." She moved so her head was resting on my
chest, took one of my hands and rested it on her right
breast. It was hard, and when I ran my finger around
the yellow scales that circled the nipple, she gave me a

little smile. I opened my mouth to say something, but closed it again. I felt hot. "And I want to see my family," she whispered.

"They must be worried sick."

"What can I do?"

"I don't know," I said. I could feel her heart beating, and when she looked at me she reached up and touched my cheek. I said, "And I don't know about this."

"I..." she said, but then she shivered.

"Isabel?"

"...think." She stiffened and a spasm shot through her body. "David..."

"What?"

"David..."

"You need some of your stuff?"

"Yes."

"Coming..."

"It's coming. It's hot... flushing."

"I'll fetch it."

"Quick, David. I need it now..."

"Half a minute..."

"Please... now..."

I ran to the kitchen, found a phial and a syringe and dashed back to the bedroom. I passed it to her, but now she was shaking and itching, and her eyes were rolling back in their sockets. She twisted her head, beat it against the pillow and started to wail. I filled the syringe, tapped the air out, found a soft place for the needle and stuck it in. She gasped and I waited, but she did not stop wailing, and the wails grew to screams, and she said she had to have more.

As the needle went in the second time she turned and gasped at me, raised her head and kissed me on my mouth. It was a light kiss, like nothing against my lips, feathers or flour drifting on a spring day. She pressed harder and I felt the tiny scales. She broke away, dropped back onto the pillow and smiled. "I feel better," she said, and closed her eyes.

I watched her for five minutes, and when she was dozing I went back to the veranda, sat down and watched the night creep around the house. It moved slowly, like it had a mind, dreams and better things to do with its time. It wanted to be away scaring children and frightening horses, or covering wooded hills. I thought about my father in his own house and how when we were a family here he used to sit with my mother and watch the marshes. And I thought about how I had just been in bed with a woman, touched a woman's breast and felt her hands on me. And although the circumstances had not matched the imaginings that had plagued some of my adolescent nights, I supposed I had passed some sort of rite. A nipple was a nipple and tumescence was tumescence, and hot breath was hot breath whatever the skin. Yes – I thought – some expectations do match the idea. And as I thought this and felt myself cool, I watched stars and the night light as it rubbed the tops of the reeds. The horizon was banked with clouds, and as I listened I heard the last gasp of

summer. The last of a warm breeze. A rustle. It turned cold
suddenly, as if everything was tumbling down. I shivered. I
shivered, crossed my arms, rubbed my shoulders, stood up
and went indoors.

In the morning the wind was blowing a gale and whistling
round the house. The walls creaked, and one of the corners
of the roof flapped. I found a hammer and nails and a ladder, climbed up and fastened a piece of loose shingle. When
I got down, Isabel was waiting for me with a cup of tea. She
was wearing a coat she had found in the wardrobe. It was
one of my father's and she had buttoned it to her chin. We
went indoors. I stoked the fire, and then we sat in the front
room and listened to the wind.

"I love it when it's like this," I said. It started to rain. "When
it's really rough it's like being on a ship."

"Good fossiling weather," she said. "There's nothing like
a good storm for stirring up the rocks."

"I don't think there're any fossils round here."

"I know there aren't." She cradled her tea in her hands and
stared at the floor. "And I don't think we can fly a kite in this."

"We could try."

"We could," she said. So when we finished our tea we
walked down to the shore again, to the place we had
been before. The sea was churning, spume filled the air
and clouds thundered over our heads. The shingle boiled
and dragged, and here and there, lumps of driftwood
upended through the surf and smashed onto the beach.

It was difficult to walk upright, but I did not try to per-
suade her to turn back. Her face was set. "Come on!"
she yelled, and our scarves whipped around our necks
and lashed at our faces.

This time I held the kite while she played out the string.
She ran away from me, lifted her arms and tugged. The kite
whipped out of my hands, flew towards the sea, doubled
backed on itself and soared back into the sky. As it climbed I
heard her laugh, and as it dipped she shouted at it to "Climb!
Climb!" – and it did as it was told.

I ran down the shingle and joined her as she played out the
last of the line. The wind sang, gave her an extra tug and almost picked her up and carried her into the waves. I grabbed
her round the waist, and we fell and tumbled towards the
surf. As we rolled, the string tangled, she let it go and the
kite climbed before stalling. It hung for a moment and then
dropped, and nothing we did could stop it. It landed on the
crest of a wave, the wave curled over and then it was gone
and we were lying on the beach together.

I shaded my eyes, but did not see the kite. "You lost it!"
I yelled.

"I'm sorry," she said, and she laughed in my ear.

"I'll have to get another."

"I really am."

"A bigger one."

We moved to a place where the shingle was banked in low
ridges and we could shelter from the worst of the weather.
We sat down; she pointed and said she could see the kite

in the waves. "There! Look!" I looked but could not see anything, and when I said it was not there she said maybe she had imagined it and her eyes were playing tricks. I said that I did not believe eyes could play tricks. "What we see," I said, "is what we see."

"Do you always think in straight lines?"

"I used to."

"Used to?"

"Until I met you."

"And what happened then?"

"I became confused," I said, and I lay back, and for a moment the sun cut through the clouds. It shone a strip of light on the waves. They foamed and beat and this time we both thought we saw the kite, but the clouds closed and the wind strengthened and it started to rain. Thin drizzle at first, but then bigger drops, and within ten minutes the sky was a solid wall of water. We started to walk away. She took my hand and squeezed it like she meant it, and I squeezed back. We had a moment in the rain, a moment that stretched and pulled and still pulls me, pulls me back to that place at that time, and then we put our heads down, shouted at the weather and ran.

We were soaked. By the time we got back to the house, Isabel was shivering and crying, but she was not unhappy. I stoked the fire, stripped off her clothes, wrapped her in towels and dry blankets, and put her to bed. She put her arms around me and said, "That was a shame."

"What was?"

"Losing the kite."

"I told you. I'm going to buy another."

"I know. But that was a special kite."

"Yes," I said, "it was." She kissed me, I kissed her, and then I went to the kitchen and put the kettle on. I stood and listened to it hiss and bubble, went to the sink and started to wash some cups. One of them was blue and the other was white. My father used to drink from the blue one, and as I was wondering how he was and what he was doing, I heard the sound of a horse on the track.

At first I thought I was imagining things, but when the hooves got closer I went outside, stepped across the veranda, down the steps and walked down the garden. The rain was still pouring, sheeting across the marshes and whipping the reeds into a frenzy. I patted the dog statue as I passed it.

The dog statue has history, a history I know and a history I do not. My father found it in Norwich, sitting outside a furniture shop with a resigned expression on its blank face, and when he asked the shop owner how much it was he was told it was not for sale.

"Not for sale?"

"You heard me."

"Then why has it got a price?"

"What are you talking about?"

My father pointed. "I'm talking about that." There was a label tied around its neck.

The man came from the shop, stared at the label and said "You must be pulling my leg. It's worth more than that."

"I don't joke," said father. It was true.

The man tore off the label, screwed it up, tossed it into the street, looked at my father and looked at me. He was bald, his face was covered in fine, veiny lines and he gave me a sympathetic look. I thought he might explode. His nose started to turn purple, and his tongue flicked out. "I wouldn't let it go for a hundred times that price," and he patted its head.

Angry and frustrated, father walked away, but after a few days he went back to the shop. This time the dog was labelled with a real price but the owner was away. His wife came out instead, and when she saw us looking at the dog she said "Make me an offer."

"Two pounds."

"I couldn't go lower than three."

"Two pounds ten."

The woman scratched her head and said, "I've wanted to get rid of it for months. Two pounds ten it is."

My father paid for the dog and was carrying it away before the woman had a chance to change her mind or her husband returned from wherever he was. "It's perfect," he said, and when we got back, I helped him carry it down the garden to a place by the pond where it could sit and watch the gate and warn visitors this was a private house.

A statue of a dog might have warned some people, but it did not worry Professor Hunt. He had tied his horse to the garden fence and now appeared at the gate, kicked it open and yelled, "And it's the librarian!" He had a bandage tied around his head and was carrying his walking stick. He swiped at the ground and the rain, and aimed a kick at some weeds.

"Hunt!"

"Thought I wouldn't find you, did you?" He walked towards me. He had not shaved for a few days, and the stubble looked like frost on his face. His eyes glittered and there was dampness around his nose. There was a large cut on his cheek and another on his hand. He was dribbling and his lips shone. "Thought I'd be too stupid to ask Mitchell's where you take your holidays?" His voice had cracks in it.

I took a few steps back. "You're not welcome here."

"Repeat?"

"You heard me."

"I'm not welcome? Is that what you said?" He cocked his ear towards me, as if he was going deaf. He could hear everything I said.

"Yes. So you'd better leave."

"Leave?" He shrugged. "You're asking me to leave without asking why I'm here?"

"I know why you're here."

"Do you?"

"Yes."

"Pray tell me – why?"

"Don't treat me like a fool."

"Why not? It's seems perfectly reasonable to…"

"She's not leaving. She's staying here."

He laughed and absent-mindedly decapitated a hollyhock with his stick. "Is she?"

"Yes."

"I see. And you'll bury her in the garden, will you?"

"What?"

"You heard me. In a week or so, when she dies, you'll bury her…"

I took a step towards him. "Go!" I yelled.

He smiled, reached up and touched the bandage around his head. "I think you two suit each other. Your tempers match…"

"Do you blame us?"

"Blame you?" He laughed. "Blame you? No. I don't think I believe in blame. It's a complete waste of time." He looked at his watch. "And I don't have much time, so if you'll tell me where she is, we'll be on our way."

"She's not here."

"But a minute ago you said she was. If you're as good a liar as you are a librarian…"

"I'm a book valuer."

"Of course you are. You put a value on art. And your art is money."

"I love books."

He spread his arms. "As all civilized people do. And maybe I should believe you, but it's difficult. I know she's here." He lifted his stick and took a step towards me.

I did not move. "And how do you know that?"

"Oh. Your eyes tell me so much." He sniffed. "And I can smell her. It's a strong smell, isn't it? Unusual…"

I shook my head. "All you can smell is the sea. And this is private property, so unless you…"

"Private property? How I wish I'd said that when you came calling on me."

"I'll call the authorities."

Now he roared with laughter. "The authorities? What authorities?"

"I'll find someone."

"I see. And when you do, what are you going to tell them?"

"I…" I said, as the door opened behind me and Isabel appeared on the veranda. She looked at me and smiled, looked at Hunt and shook her head, and Hunt said, "Ah…" She shrugged, arranged the scarf around her neck and walked down the steps.

She moved like a princess in a fabulous dress making an entrance down a grand staircase, with smartly dressed people waiting and music playing. The wind is beating against the windows, but the windows are secure, and rain is falling on people who stand outside and wait. Leaves ripped from trees, candles burning on tables, waiters carrying trays of drinks. Carriages sweeping up a long drive, liveried men opening doors. The gentle burble of conversation, the smell of delicate food. She held the coat tightly around her, and when she reached the bottom of the steps she stopped, looked at Hunt and said, "Back so soon?"

"I couldn't keep away."

"And how is your head?"

"Stronger than you'd think," he said.

"That's a shame."

He touched the bandage again. "Geniuses have stronger skulls than other people. It's a well-known fact."

"Is it?"

"Absolutely," he said, and he flailed his stick, pushed past me and ran towards her.

I remember his face – full of anger and expectation and pride – and I remember hers – calm and scaled and hating – and I remember hearing birds through the rain – terns, I think. They made squeaking sounds, and sounds like distant guns firing, then more squeaks. And the rustle of the reeds layered the terns like music from a long time ago, when I did not have the sort of worries I have now. And I thought I heard a string quartet playing something slow and stately, something composed by a man who should have worn a wig but did not. A beautiful melody, a quiet section, the melody returned.

Isabel pulled a kitchen knife from her coat a moment before he reached her. I looked at it, not with surprise or shock but with curiosity, an object out of its element, like someone reading a book in a rain storm or a horse smoking a cigarette. She looked at him and he could not stop himself. He was running too fast, and as he ran onto the blade his expression changed in exactly the way you would expect. He looked totally surprised and gave a gasp of astonishment. His eyes widened. His tongue popped out of his mouth, then popped back in. His head tipped to one side. He looked at her, looked at me, looked back at her, looked down at his stomach, gripped the knife and sank to his knees.

"There," she said, and she sank with him and for a moment they looked as though they were locked in embrace, two lovers in the rain who would not break apart. She whispered something in his ear and stood up. As she did she twisted the knife and pulled it in a curve from his belly to his chest. Blood spread across his shirt; he gasped and wheezed. His eyes stayed wide, frozen and glaring, and his tongue stuck out. His lips peeled back and all his teeth shone at me, yellow at the back and whiter in front. She gave a tug, stood back and dropped the knife.

"Isabel!" I ran to her, but she stepped away and headed back to the house. "Isabel!" She did not turn or say anything. She climbed the steps, crossed the veranda and slammed the door behind her. As it banged I waited for the glass to break, but it did not. It stayed in the frame and the terns called again.

I went to Hunt. He was still kneeling, his head bowed, and he was making a low gurgling sound. I touched his shoulder and he tipped over and lay on the grass. The knife was under his knee, and blood was pulsing from his belly and pooling around him. He opened his mouth and tried to say something, but spat more blood. His eyes had lost their glare and looked something like a child's eyes, innocent and uncomprehending and waiting for something they could not imagine. I felt faint and sick, and all my nerves were singing under my skin. My nose was clogging and I said "You…" but could not think of the next word.

"She…" he said, and he made a sound like a ball bursting. His eyes closed, a trickle of blood ran from the corner of his mouth and his right leg gave one last twitch. I waited, but he did not move again, and when I looked up my house was quiet and still, the curtains closed, the door shut, the veranda empty.

I sat on the lawn for half an hour. I stared at the body as it seeped on the lawn. It wheezed for a while, but then went quiet. The rain did not stop. It pattered on the coat, soaked through to the skin and washed the blood into the grass. As I stared, I breathed steadily and thought carefully. I did not panic. I thought methodically, running through the things I would have to do one at a time, then going back and starting again.

I did not want to go to prison and wait a few months for my trial and listen to lies or half-truths, and I did not want to face the judge as he slipped the black cap on his head and lowered his eyes at me. I did not want to sit in a cell and brood, and I did not want to die on a gallows. I did not want any of these things to happen, and so I did not panic. It is difficult to get rid of a body when the first time you have to get rid of a body is the first time you see one. A dead body with a terrible knife wound. A murder. I did not want to go to prison. I was wet. Murder is a terrible crime.

So I took precise, deliberate steps. I wished I knew the game of chess, but I did not. I wished I knew about climbing mountains, about the careful steps climbers take. I thought about books I had read. Books where people who did not want to but were forced to had to get rid of bodies they were not responsible for and did not want in their bedrooms, barns, gardens or fields. I remembered the stories, but could not remember what they were called or who wrote them. Usually I am good at remembering titles and authors. I have to be, but in my garden I was not.

First, I fetched his horse. It was standing where he had tied it, head down, dripping, steaming from its flanks. I led it around the back of the house to the barn, opened the spare stable door and tapped it inside. It snorted at my horse, but was grateful for the dry. Then I led my own horse to the gig, harnessed it and whispered in its ear. I had heard that horses know English but cannot understand a word of French or German. "Wait a minute," I said. "I'll be back."

I went to the garden shed, chose a spade from the wall, put it in the gig and then went back to the garden. I felt sick. I gagged. I held myself in, took a deep breath and pulled Hunt across the grass, through one of the flower beds and some of the borders and onto the path. He was heavy, and the rain made the job difficult, and when I reached the gig I had to heave him up like a sack of rocks and push him onto the seat with my feet. As I pushed him, little popping noises came from his nose, and he groaned. I jumped, fell out and landed on my back. The rain did not stop. I opened my mouth, let it fill with water and stood up. He did not groan again, but he started to leak. He leaked on the seat and floor, slime, water and blood. The horse started to whinny and stamp, so I soothed it again, and then went indoors.

Isabel was sitting in the kitchen. She had blood on her hands and my father's coat was covered in blood, and blood was on the floor. She said, "Is he dead?"

I nodded.

"It's a lot of death."

"Yes," I said, and I went to the bathroom and washed my hands. I went to the bedroom and packed some fresh clothes in a bag – trousers, a shirt, a pullover and a coat. When I came back I said, "I'm going for a drive." I looked at my watch. "I'll be an hour or two. Maybe longer."

"Where are you going?"

"Where do you think?"

"I don't know, David! I can't read your mind!"

"I'm going to get rid of him!" I pointed out of the window. She looked at the gig. "And while I'm doing that, you can clean the mess up!" I pointed to the blood on the floor. "And you can give me that!" I pointed at my father's coat.

She ripped it off. A button popped, flew across the room and clattered against the window. She threw it at me, ran to the bedroom and slammed the door. I stood and held my father's coat in my hands, put it to my nose and smelt the edge of something he had once said to me. Something about being true to yourself and never allowing pain to take you over. And then I thought about yelling something at the bedroom door – but I did not, and I left without pouring two cups of tea and fetching some biscuits.

* * *

How many times in your life do you find yourself with a leaking corpse in a gig? Never. Or, if you are unlucky, once. And if you are unluckier, you think too much about what you have to do. You think and your thoughts crinkle at the edges, gather in the centre and end up pulling at the loose ends of your mind. Your mind spins out and the bits wrinkle until they spill. You pull in the opposite direction but it does not help. It does not help at all, but maybe you did not want it to. Maybe all you wanted was sleep, and the poor desperate love you felt drowned like roughed feathers in ink.

I drove west, through Blakeney, towards Wells. The wind was still blowing, but the rain had stopped. The clouds raced, and here and there streaks of lit blue sky showed through. I drove carefully, and concentrated on not thinking. I did not think about Hunt and I did not think about Isabel, and I did not think about the time when I used to be pleased and thought I was so clever. I did not think about my father and his reading. Nothing could make me shift my focus. Everything I saw seemed bright and clear and sharp. A bird. Another bird, brown with white wings and a crest on its head. And I was calm. I surprised myself, but not enough to make me jump.

I had propped Hunt so he looked asleep, covered him with my father's old coat and laid a blanket over that. I did not look at him. I looked straight ahead and breathed. When I reached Wells, I kept my head down, but everyone I saw was walking with their backs bent and their own heads down, or hiding from the weather. Shop canopies flapped, signs were swinging and wet birds huddled in rows.

A few ~~miles beyond~~ Holkham there was a bend in the road. I slowed down until I found a narrow track that ran into the damp land between the verge and the sea. It was not marked or signposted – if you passed it at speed you would not notice it – but I remembered it from the previous year. I turned off the main road and drove down the track until I reached a kink where it split in two, and this second track disappeared into the marshes, narrowed, twisted and dropped into a hidden dip.

I stopped the horse in the middle of the dip and stared at a curtain of reeds. A few spots of rain blew into my face. I turned and looked at Hunt. His head had slipped out of the blanket, blood had dribbled onto the floor, and even dead he did not look relaxed. He looked as though he was taking a break between angry sentences and would sit up in a minute, wipe the blood from his mouth and shout something about fools.

"All right," I said to him, but he did not move or say anything. "Are you ready?" Nothing.

I heard a carriage on the main road – the wind, the drag of waves on the shingle, bird calls. Once I had wanted to identify every bird I saw, but now I was not bothered, because all the birds I wanted to know anything about had flown away. All my senses were tuned like needles to what I was doing there. I felt no panic or alarm. The noise of the carriage faded away, the smell of mud and salt rose in the wind, and the taste of salt filled my mouth.

I jumped down from my seat and stepped into a puddle. I cursed, spat and then I pulled Hunt down and laid him in the mud. There was blood everywhere, and I said a word of regret to my father's coat. Regret is, I suppose, inevitable, but I did not like to think about it, dwell on it or wonder. There was no time.

I took the spade and went to the middle of the dip of land, and I started to dig. I suppose you could say I was lucky, for the sods came away easily, and the ground was soft. I worked for half an hour and had the grave about three feet deep when the sides started to collapse, and water started to fill the bottom. There was nothing I could do, so I carried on, heaving the mud out and piling it in a ridge above me.

At some point – I have no idea when – a break appeared in the clouds, and a thin cut of sunlight fell on the marshes. As it crept towards me, I stopped digging and watched, and made some sort of connection between the sky and dead Professor Hunt. I do not know, but maybe madness is contagious and I had caught a dose. I was not going to let it touch me, so when the sunlight faded away and the clouds rubbed the place where it had been, I went back to my digging, deeper and deeper until I thought I was six feet down.

How does a grave-digger climb out of his graves? A ladder, I suppose. I propped the spade against the side, stepped onto its handle and hauled myself out, lay down, picked the spade out and looked at my work. Maybe it was too narrow, but

I had no choice and no time. I stepped to Hunt's body and, without stopping to think, put my foot against his waist and pushed him in. He rolled easily and dropped into the grave. He stuck about two foot down, his arms jammed against the sides. There was nothing I could do, so I took the spade and smashed it against his shoulders until he fell to the bottom, his head twisted to one side, his arms splayed and his legs crooked. He looked less like a dead man, more like a collection of parts someone had put together and left to rot.

Now I stripped off my clothes, tossed them over the body and changed into the clean trousers and shirt and jacket. Then, aching and tired and feeling desperate with fear and more fear, I started to shovel the earth back. As the first clods hit the body, they made sickening thuds, and as the weight of earth started to push down, I heard the last wheeze of the man's death. I can hear it now – a low, lonely whisper, something from the hell he made, and I had to walk away and empty my guts before going back and finishing the awful work.

Nothing was out of place. I laid the broken sods over the grave and spread reeds around, and when I stepped back, even the marshes looked right, the way they waved in the breeze and the way birds rustled through them to the sea. I went back to the gig, whipped the horse around and started to drive away from the place, eyes right and left, right and left, and then I was on the main road and clipping back towards Holkham with the wind at my back and the sting of the first drops of a new storm on my neck.

I do not know how long it took me to get home, but I did not stop, did not look over my shoulder and did not care when my clothes were soaked with freezing rain and I felt my muscles chattering. I just pushed the horse on, head down, through the marshes, down the road, around the bend, into Holkham, through Holkham, out of Holkham and into Wells. I wanted to stop, I wanted a cup of tea, a plate of biscuits and a view through a steamed window, but my eyes would not let me stop. I looked ahead.

As I was taking the road from town, my heart began to scream. It started quietly, but by the time I could see the track to my place it was bursting my ears and twisting in my chest. It scraped like a wheel against a rock, going nowhere but wishing to be everywhere at once, from a place on a warm beach to a seat beside a gentle Scottish river. A florist's stall on Leather Lane, bookshops on the Charing Cross Road, a mews house in Stoke Newington. A little public house in Edinburgh. Places my heart wanted – and it screamed louder; I put my head down, gasped, turned onto my track and stopped. I fell out of the gig, collapsed in the mud, opened my mouth and let the rain fill me. My heart skipped, and stopped for a moment. I lay back and listened to my body think about dying. It thought for a second. I heard it whisper to my feet, and my feet moved. My heart kicked in my chest and I took a huge, gasping breath. Water fountained out of my mouth. I looked towards my house. It looked quiet and waiting. The marshes thrashed and sucked, and when I was ready I stood up again, unhitched the horse, led it to the stable and piled some hay in the crib. I went back to the gig. The rain had washed most of Hunt's blood away, but I tossed some buckets of water on the stains that remained, wiped them clean with a cloth and went indoors.

The sweet sickly smell hit me as soon as I walked in. Isabel was sitting by the fire, her head between her knees. The kitchen table was covered in the smashed remains of phials, and the stuff she had to inject was dripping on the floor.

"Isabel?"

"What?"

"What has happened?"

"My grandmother used to tell me – never put off until tomorrow what you can do today."

I went to the table, dipped my fingers in the stuff and sniffed them. "Oh God."

"And she was a wise woman."

"What have you done?"

"What does it look like?"

"But I thought we were going to wait until we had word from William. We were going to…"

"You thought, David, and that's all it was. A thought. I said nothing." I went to the sink and washed my face and hands. It made no difference. I couldn't get the smell off my skin. When I came back she said, "And what did you do with him?"

"I buried him."

She smiled. "Good."

"What did you do with the knife?"

"It's in there." She pointed to the fire.

I picked up a poker, sifted through the ashes and found the blade. It had turned blue and grey, and the handle had burned away. I pulled it out, picked it up with the tongs and took it outside. As I stepped off the veranda, the rain hissed on the metal. I dunked it in a water butt, carried it to the shed, wrapped it in a bag and hid it in a gap between the roof and the walls. When I went back to the house, I started to spoon some of the potion off the table into an egg cup. Before she had a chance to ask me what I was doing I said, "I'm not giving up."

She stood up, smashed the egg cup out of my hand, fetched the kettle from the stove and splashed water over the table. The substance diluted and ran away in streams. She filled the kettle again and poured it over the remains, said "I have" and went to the bedroom. I heard the bed springs go and the sound of sheets rustling. I followed her, sat on a chair by my mother's dressing table and said "So that's it, is it?"

"Yes."

"You want to die?"

"Yes."

"Why?"

"Because it's pointless. Useless. I'm a freak, I'm going blind, I've killed someone and I hurt everywhere."

"You're going blind?"

"Yes."

"You didn't tell me that."

She shrugged. "Everything's going pale. I feel like I'm looking at things through milk."

"I don't want you to die."

"And you have a say in this?"

"I saved you."

"Saved me?" She laughed. "I don't think you did."

"I helped you get away from Hunt."

"And what good did that do?"

"I... you..."

"Yes?"

"You flew a kite."

"Oh yes," she said. "Oh yes." She rolled the words around her mouth like they were food, and her eyes softened towards me. "The kite. Thank you for that."

I was going to say something else, but did not bother. I went outside, stood in the sodden garden and stared at the place where Hunt had died. The rain had turned to a whipping drizzle, and the daylight was fading as I walked out of the gate and into the reeds, down to the shore and the place where we had flown the kite. The sea fumed, the shingle crashed and the sails of a distant ship winked through the spray. I looked west and I looked east, and suddenly all my weaknesses collapsed around me. I watched them fail, crumble and die, and I sat down, put my head between my knees and felt that nothing mattered any more, nothing in London or in Norfolk, or in my head as I turned and spun and let the sea smash me down to the end.

The storm was failing in the morning, and when I sat up in bed and listened I could hear the shingle being pulled and torn as if it was the edge of a dress in a fight. I turned and looked at Isabel, and she looked at me. She had cried in the night, cried at herself and me and the weather, and now she said, "Was I ungrateful?"

"Maybe," I said.

"I'm sorry if I was."

"You've got much to be ungrateful about."

"I've got more than much to be ungrateful about." She stretched out her arms and rubbed them together. A few scales dropped off her elbow.

"I know."

"And I want to see my grandmother," she said, and she turned away from me, buried her head in her pillow and whispered, "Grandmother... I wanted to help her."

"I know," I said, but my words were foolish and weak, so I went to make a pot of tea. As I stood at the window I looked north, waited for the water to boil and waited for retribution. I waited and I lived and listened to the wind finger at the place I had mended on the roof. It was working its way under the felting and trying to pop the nails. This place – I thought – this place does not need to be made from wood and nails, but this place is. And this place – I thought – does not need to hold us like a fist.

I made the tea, took her a cup and said "I've got to go out today."

"Where?"

"I don't know. I've just got to get away from this place."

"I'll come," she said.

"If you want."

We dressed without talking, and while I fetched the horse and harnessed the gig, she stared at the sky and wept. We were desperate and sad, angry and silent.

I did not drive fast. When we reached Salthouse, I whipped the horse past the houses and carried on to Weybourne, and when we were past Weybourne I drove on to Sheringham. I took the road to Pretty Corner, and when we reached a clearing I stopped and we sat and looked down from the ridge to the sea, and watched the waves rolling in. The sun broke through the clouds and spread shafts of bright, clean light on the world, and as birds came out to sing we went for a walk.

She wore her coat, a scarf and boots, and as we walked she took my arm. She squinted at the path and rubbed her eyes. "Why can't I see?" she said, but I did not have an answer for her.

The woods were thick and wet. Beech, birch, ash and fir trees covered the ridge, damp dead leaves were deep along the path, and the air was dark with regret. There were places we passed that reminded me of places I had seen in Somerset, but I did not say anything. Maybe Isabel was reminded of somewhere in Dorset, a place where she used to play when she was small, but she did not say anything either. Only the pad of our footsteps, the call of late birds and the last gasps of the storm disturbed the silence, and when we reached a clearing with a view of the ocean we sat down on a fallen log.

The waves rolled in and the clouds swirled over our heads, and after a few minutes she said, "When I was five, I found something in woods like this."

"What?"

"We were on holiday in Cornwall, staying in a cottage on the side of a hill. Mother and Father love walking, and it was lovely there. We used to go out every day. One day they found a forest trail." She pointed down the path. "I ran on ahead." She squinted at the path. "I always used to do that."

"So did I."

"I remember... I came to this clearing. There was a little stream I had to jump across, and a circle of trees. I could hear Mother calling for me, but I didn't stop walking until I was in the middle of the clearing. There were flowers growing in the grass, little yellow ones shaped like stars. I sat down and started picking some. I wanted to make a posy..." She stopped, turned and looked at me. A fly had landed on her forehead. It was walking across the scales, picking at the gaps between them. I reached up to brush it away and said, "And?"

"I found a dying bird. A blackbird. It was lying in a puddle. Its eyes were glassy and it was making little wheezing sounds, trying to flap its wings, but it knew..."

"Knew what?"

"That it was dying. I wanted to pick it up and take it home, and try and nurse it back to life, but Mother told me to leave it where it was. I think that was the first moment, the moment

I knew I wanted to do some good in the world. Or at least try. I remember… I bent down and picked it up and held it in my hands, and as I did, it lifted its head up, blinked at me and made a little squeak. It was trying to sing, trying to sing its last song. Then… then it died…" Her voice stalled, she put her hands over her eyes and she took a heaving sob of a breath. She looked back at me, and her face was covered in tears. I gave her a handkerchief, and while she dabbed at her cheeks she said, "It died in my hands."

"I'm sorry," I said.

"I was too," she said, and as we sat in silence for a few minutes the rustling trees seemed to quieten over us, and the waves below slowed.

"I…" I started, but she interrupted.

"When will they find him?"

I shook my head. "I don't know. Maybe never. I dug deep, and the place is hidden."

She picked up a stick and started poking in the ground. "And how long before they come calling?"

"Who are they?"

"The police."

I shrugged. "They might never."

She drew a figure of eight, put a cross through it and whispered, "I'm scared."

"So am I."

"I didn't think…"

"Did he? Did he ever really think?"

"All the time," she said, "but never about the right things."

"Did he have any family?"

She shook her head. "Not that I heard of. But he never said anything about that side of his life."

I wanted to say something about blame, but now I was tired and I wanted to lie down. She tossed her stick into the air, and as it arced into the undergrowth I stood up. A bank of dark cloud was looming over the horizon, and the light was turning pink. I said, "It's going to rain," she said, "Never…" and we started to walk back to the gig. A bolt of lightning flashed behind us, thunder rumbled by, and we had just started to move when it began to tip with rain.

As we were passing through Sheringham, we saw a wedding party leaving a church. The bride and groom were standing in the porch, staring at the rain. Guests were clustering around, some in worried groups behind the happy couple, others not caring, soaked to the skin and laughing. I had to slow down while the wedding carriage pulled into the kerb, and as I passed it, one of the guests looked up at Isabel. Her scarf had slipped down and, as he saw her, his face changed from angry to panic like a season, his jaw dropped and he tried to shout. Nothing came out. He turned and pointed at us, but before anyone could join him we were away and the groom was picking the bride up and carrying her across the sodden pavement, and the bridesmaids were screaming and laughing.

"Have you ever been married?" said Isabel.

"No."

"Do you want to be?"

I shrugged and said I did not know.

"I'll take that to mean no," she said, and she wrapped a blanket around her shoulder, turned her head away from me and watched the weather through her milky, fading eyes. She watched, and I watched, and we watched together, and as we did I felt something snap in the air. I do not know if she heard it too, but she did close her eyes and rest her head on my shoulder, and as we rattled home she started to make little rasping noises in her throat, as if insects were trapped in there and all they wanted to do was escape.

It ended in the night. The wind dropped and the rain stopped and an odd stillness hung in the air. The smell of grass and salt caught in my throat, and shy birds called. I poured a whisky, and as I drank I followed its burn, felt it settle, poured another and went to sit on the veranda to drink. I stared into the dark and counted the stars, but their distance or mystery meant nothing to me. They could have burst and cried before me, but I would not have worried. Mystery is swallowed by guilt – guilt the worst punch in the jaw and all the rest. When I finished the whisky, I went to bed.

We slept together. She was quiet for a couple of hours, but at around three o'clock she started to shiver and moan in her sleep. The blankets had slipped off, so I got up, pulled them back, spread them over her and climbed back into bed, but it did not make any difference. The shivers did not go away.

Ten minutes later she woke, sat up and whined. I looked up at her. Her breath was steaming and there was foam around her mouth. I got up, drew a glass of water, held it to her lips, and she tried to drink but could not swallow. She spat it across the room and slumped back, gripped the sheets and gasped. Shudders broke through her body. I put my arms around her and tried to hold her, but she pushed me away. Her legs thrashed, the whining got louder and she let out the first scream.

There are screams and there are screams. There are screams of delight when people hear of success, screams of shock when virgins see the shadow of a monster climbing up their bedroom walls. Screams of hate and screams of pain. Screams to shatter glass or break china, and screams as old trees split and fall through gales. More screams than types of food or mineral. Isabel's scream came from deep, welled up, broke out and shook the house. The windows rattled in their frames, and the cups and plates on the draining board slid into the sink. Her eyes popped, and she opened her mouth so wide I thought she was going to dislocate her jaw.

It was so loud I wanted to scream back, and when she took a breath for the next, she dropped her head between her knees, arched her back, heaved, reached up and let it tear from her body. She hit her arms and hit her legs and ran her nails across her stomach. A sour, bad smell started to fill the room. She turned over, struggled to reach a place on her back, failed, tried again and then fell back. She lay perfectly still for a moment, her eyes wide open and her breathing slow. I put my hand on her forehead and said, "Ssh..." She did not blink or look at me, but then she heaved again, whispered, "If you knew how much…" but she did not finish the sentence. She took a deep breath, clutched at her stomach and screamed again, thrashed, turned and rolled off the bed.

I jumped up and went to where she was lying. I tried to turn her over, but she pushed me away, rubbing and scratching at the skin, twisting and buckling. "It's crawling," she wailed. "Crawling. I've got insects. Too many insects. Biting…"

"What?"

"Millions of insects. They're biting. I should have some stuff… I need it…" She slapped her arms, the smell got worse, I pulled a sheet off the bed and laid it over her. She screamed as it touched her, ripped it away and threw it back at me. She yelled, "No!" rolled over, smashed against the door, rolled back, hit my legs and then stopped. She stiffened, let out a long, wheezing sigh and then, like a bird settling on its nest, stilled.

I sat in a chair by the bed and watched her. She was breathing slowly, each breath making a quiet buzz in her throat. Her eyes were closed, but they twitched behind their lids. When she started to shiver I picked her up, laid her on the bed and spread the sheets over her. This time she did not throw them off but tucked her knees to her chin and made little weepy noises. I whispered "I'll be in the kitchen" in her ear and left her alone.

I poured a glass of whisky. It was half-past three. I stood at the bedroom door and watched her for five minutes. She was sleeping now, lying flat on her back and wheezing quietly. I left the door open and went back to the kitchen, sat down and drank.

I drank and thought about bodies burning, organs popping and guilt. I thought about good things I had done and bad things, and I asked big questions. Can murder ever be justified? Do animals have a sense of humour? Did Voltaire prefer the society of men? How many cups of tea can you safely drink in a day? What's the difference between a banana? What does your body do with protein? I asked these questions but did not answer them. I was tired but knew I would never sleep, and when Isabel stirred and called my name, I went to sit by her again. I ran the tips of my fingers over the scales around her eyes and held her hand.

I was going to ask her how she felt, but before I could open my mouth she started wailing more and then screaming and thrashing, yelling about the crawling under her skin being worse, the insects having sharper teeth and she being unable to live any more here or anywhere she could think of or I might suggest. She did not want to live any more and wanted me to hold her hand as she died. I told her I would hold her hand for as long as she wanted and would not leave her unless she told me to, and the lights she could see in her eyes were not lights outside but came from inside, and she was not to worry, she was not going to die. She sat up, took long, heaving breaths, struggled to find words, yelled "Ants!" and fell back again. Scratched her arms and legs, ripped her fingernails across her stomach and tore some scales away. "Can't!" she screamed. I put my arms around her; she pushed me away and pulled me back. She buried her head in my shoulder. I gagged at her smell, twisted my neck and thought I heard something, something coming towards me, hissing and puffing, and I think it was a railway train, a railway train whispering over the horizon towards my place.

I thought I heard a railway train as I held on to Isabel, and I thought I saw the first twist of smoke through a forest, layers of smoke settling on the trees, and then it broke out of the shade and came towards me.

At first, like some things are, it was silent and black and white. I did not recognize it. I thought it was just a train and the carriages were filled with people. There were lovers, businessmen, children, a priest, a party of doctors and people just travelling one stop. Some were talking and others were quiet, and some were smoking. There were leather straps on the doors: you had to pull them down to open the window. And in first class there were antimacassars on the seats and a vague smell of brandy.

As the train got nearer, the driver leant out of his cab. He had a blackened face and wore dark-blue overalls and a ragged cap. He pulled on a rope, the train whistled and birds blew out of trees and hedges. Sheep bolted, and in one of the carriages someone lit a pipe.

I smelt the tobacco, and then the thing I thought was a train was on top of me and steam was clouding up, but it was not really a train. It was Isabel screaming again, howling, lashing out at me, scrabbling at her skin, trying to rip it off, digging her fingernails into her thighs. Her eyes were spinning. Her tongue flipped back and she started to choke. I tried to get my fingers into her mouth but she bit them, grabbed my hand, pulled it away and kicked me off the bed.

I rolled across the floor, banged against the door and blacked out. I do not know how long I was out, but when I came to I felt blood trickling down the back of my head. I sat up and then stood up. She was lying back. I took a step towards her, she tried to sit her up. Blood was seeping from breaks in the scales on her arms and legs. She opened her mouth, managed half a word, slumped back and turned away from me. I sat on the edge of the bed and spread my fingers across her back.

Her shoulder blades were like wings folded beneath her skin, and as I stared at them I thought all I had to do was take a knife and release those wings and she would have freedom. I could have folded the flaps of skin, and feathers could have grown from her blood, as if her blood was magic and I had a greater power. Her bones might have clicked and spread and sung along their edges, and my knife could have sung in return, but it did not.

I ran my fingers over those hidden wings and kissed the back of her neck. She twitched and buried her head in the pillow. She blinked and her eyes filled with tears. She opened her mouth, said nothing, stared and then she dropped away from me like a stone. I reached out and tried to grab her, but her breath failed, her eyes rolled back and she gave one last sigh, like an echo over a mountain in the summer.

I sat with her until the dawn broke, lines of light oozed into the dark and the first birds called. Then I straightened her on the bed, and as the colour began to drain from her scales, I washed the blood away and laid a fresh sheet over her. I pulled it up to her neck, stroked her face, spread my arms and laid on her. I hugged her, buried my face in her neck and took a deep breath of her smell. She was hard and cold against me, and when I stood up again dimples patterned my face. I pulled the sheet up and covered her completely, and I left her like that. I turned off the lights and stood alone for a few minutes. I was empty. When I was ready, I walked to the shore.

I walked through the marshes. The light was brighter now, milky and blue and pale together. I could feel the way. It was flat. I heard the reeds, and the sea came washing after the storm.

When I reached the beach I walked towards the place where we had flown the kite and looked for it, but I did not see it. I looked carefully. I am a careful man. That's my job. I could be a railway driver. I like railways. I could be a fisherman. I like boats.

I thought random thoughts as I walked, all the way to the ridges of shingle. I sat down.

I stared at the waves as the sun rose through a low hedge of cloud, and light exploded across the sea. I blinked and shaded my eyes, and all the birds blew into life. They rose behind me and flew away. I could go for a long walk, a trip across Europe to Istanbul or Tashkent. I could take my savings and use them to do good in a poor country. Or I could do exactly the same things I have always done, make no plans and be vaguely pleased.

I sat and, as the sun climbed, tiredness crept up and flooded my body. I stood up, turned my back on the sea and walked away, and when I reached the marshes I did not stop to listen to the bitterns as they crept through the reeds, and when I reached my house I did not pat the statue of a dog as I walked up the garden, and as I climbed the steps and crossed the veranda I did not hear a sound from inside, or from the skies that rolled over my head.

Dorset

I stayed in Norfolk for a while. The place held me in its arms and I rested my head on its shoulders. I felt its breath, its sadness and an unexpected happiness. I whispered to it, and if I listened carefully I could hear it whispering back. Real words, soothing me and letting me know it loved me, wanted me to stay, wanted to give me gifts.

When I felt able, I wrote the beginning of this book and some of the rest, and when I finished I put the pages in a folder and drank three glasses of whisky. I slept for twelve hours. When I woke up I left the house without looking back, hitched my horse to the gig, tied Hunt's horse to the back and drove away.

I was empty. Autumn was bad, and that melancholy time was thick with leaves and wind. I drove away from the flat lands. I said goodbye to the one horse at Norwich and rode Hunt's on to London. I left it tied to a graveyard fence near Blackheath. I patted its side, nodded to a beautiful woman with blond hair I saw walking across the heath and then walked the few miles to Highbury. The city was blank and cold, and people were wearing their coats. I came upon a scrawny dog. It followed me for a while, yapping and sniffing at my heels, but he left me before I crossed the river. I think he was afraid to leave the south of the city, afraid of the water and the sky. I was not. I stood on Southwark Bridge and watched the swell and current for five minutes, and the rubbish as it swilled. The barges and lighters were busy, and so were the tugs.

I walked on. I called at my rooms to collect my letters. I stood in my kitchen and watched the lovely tree in the garden next door, but it failed me. Its tumbling leaves meant nothing, and the birds were dumb. I washed, changed into fresh clothes, left my rooms, locked the door and walked to my office.

I spoke to Mr Hick. I had made a decision. I did not tell him what I needed to say, but I told him I would be back at my desk within the week. There were a few things I had to sort out, and he said that was fine; he had had a chance to see some of the Buff-Orpington collection, the Dresden *Œuvres* really were as good as I had said, and the Chairman wanted to meet me. He was very pleased with my work, and there was an excellent chance I would be invited to his estate for Christmas. "Do you know what this could mean?" he said. I said I did not, but could guess, and as I left the offices, I thought – once again – that maybe I would never see them again. Maybe now really was the time to leave one life and find another.

My earlier wanderings had given me a taste for the aimless, so I walked the streets for an hour or more, and as the day crept through the afternoon towards evening, I decided to call on Timothy. When I reached his rooms, I banged on the door but got no reply. I called his name, and as I was turning to leave, a door on the landing above opened, and a man in shirtsleeves appeared. He demanded to know what the noise was about. When I explained I was looking for my old friend, I was told the unthinkable but inevitable. Timothy was no longer there. He had fallen in love with an actress, and was living in the gardens opposite the Sadler's Wells theatre, watching and waiting for the object of his obsession.

I was tired and needed to sleep, so I returned to my rooms, and after a long night of sweats and nightmares, I set out to find him as dawn broke, away from Highbury, down stirring Upper Street, over the Angel to the theatre. I stopped for a hot cup of tea at a stall on Chadwell Street. I asked the woman who stirred the pot if she knew of someone who was living on the rough in the area. She laughed and said, "Go to the churchyard," and pointed up the road. "There's a dozen up there. A dozen more on Exmouth Market." She waved her hands. "And that's for starters."

I thanked her and drank the tea. It was hot and sweet, and when I headed towards the churchyard I felt it swilling in my stomach and, like rabid bats, my thoughts began to thrash blindly against the inside of my skull. When I found the tramps of the yard, still tossing and mumbling in their drunk sleep, I stepped amongst them, staring into their failed faces, seeing no one, no Timothy, no old friend of mine sunk so distant and mad, so far from promise and ambition. I retraced my steps, turned back towards Sadler's Wells, and when I reached the theatre, took my starting point from the stage door.

On the far side of the road was a row of tall houses, all fronted with gardens – some smart, some overgrown. I approached the first, looked over the wall, and called his name. "Timothy?" There was no reply, so I walked to the next, and the next, and the next, calling all the time, parting the branches of the bushes and trees and peering down. At one house, curtains twitched and a man's sleepy face appeared. He stared at me, opened the window and shouted out, "What do you think you're doing?"

"Looking for a friend."

"Well he's not here," said the man, "so get on with you," and he slammed the window and watched as I made my way farther down the road to a small park.

I strolled through the fallen leaves, around a couple of weedy flower beds and a pigeoned statue. I was beginning to experience the woolly feeling I get if I rise too early, and was thinking about returning home when I found him. He was sleeping on the grass beneath a bench, covered in a soiled coat, with a brown woollen hat on his head and a scarf around his neck. For a moment I thought I had simply found another tramp, but when I said his name, he stirred and I recognized his eyes. They were hidden in a face that had changed from the one I'd known in Edinburgh. He had a rough beard and a livid scar that disfigured his forehead, and his lips were rough and peeling, but his eyes were still blue and almost bright. I crouched down and put my hand to his shoulder. He flinched.

"Timothy?"

"Who's there?"

"David. David Morris."

He sat up, leant on the bench and squinted at me. I thought he was going to smile, but he did not. He simply shook his head and said, "Do I know you?"

"Yes," I said. "We're friends."

He almost laughed. "I have no friends."

"Yes you do."

Now his eyes flared, and he scratched his beard and raised his voice. "No! I have none," and he hauled himself to his feet, staggered, reached out and turned. I stood and tried to put my hand on his arm, but he brushed me off and started to walk away. He stopped and looked towards the theatre, and a terrible look swept across his face. I thought he was going to cry, to break down and confess something to me, but his mouth hardened and he said, "No friends, no one."

"Timothy?"

He looked at me, and now I think he recognized me. I think he remembered how we had been friends, and I think he saw us in the streets and bars of Edinburgh, talking about fathers and futures and books, and he stopped. "David?" he said. "Maybe I do remember a David."

"Good," I said, and I put my hand on his arm again, and said, "Can I buy you a cup of tea?"

He thought about this, looked towards the theatre again and said, "I'm waiting for someone."

"I know you are," I said, "but I'm sure you've got time for an old friend."

A half-smile crept onto his face, he looked down at my hand and said, "I would enjoy something hot."

"Then come with me," I said, and we walked down towards Exmouth Market, and found a steamy café with little tables and a friendly woman who brought us our tea and some bacon rolls.

Timothy ate as though he had not eaten for days, and when he had finished, I bought him another roll, and he ate that just as quickly. Then he took some tea, leant back, loosened his coat and said, "I was hungry."

I drank some of my tea. "What happened to you? What happened to the novel?"

"What novel?"

"The one you were writing."

"Oh, that one." He looked at me, looked at the floor, looked towards the window and then looked back at me. "It's over."

"What do you mean?"

"I found another interest."

"A woman?"

"Oh yes," he said, "a woman," and a mad splinter cut his right eye. "A beautiful woman."

"Who is she?"

"Barbara. She's an actress."

"And you think you're going to impress her by sleeping under a park bench?"

"I don't want to impress her."

"No?"

"I just want to love her."

"Of course you do," I said.

"And I want her to love me."

"So what are you going to do?"

"Wait for her. Wait for her to understand."

"And what would your father think about that?"

"I don't know. Nor do I care. He's washed his hands of me."

I shook my head, drank some tea, watched him drink his and said, "You can't give up."

"I know."

"Then go home, clean yourself up, find a fresh shirt…"

He held his hand up. "Home? Shirt?" he said.

"Yes."

He almost smiled, and now I realized I was wasting my time. Friendship cannot be friendship without honesty. It crawls away, hides behind a rock and peeps out from behind its fingers. I said, "I think you're a coward."

"I don't care what you think."

"Admit it, Timothy. There was a time when you'd have agreed with me. Not that you'd remember."

"I remember," he said, "and when I look at you, look at what you've done, I thank God I am who I am. I never wanted your sort of life. I mean to say, do you ever ask yourself what you really want? Do you ever look in the mirror and think, 'I don't want this grey face, this grey work, this grey place?'"

"I…"

"I'm free, David."

"Free to spend your days obsessing about a woman you'll never have?"

"At least I obsess about something."

"And you know I don't?"

"Now you're contradicting yourself," he said, and he swallowed the last of his tea, stood up, pushed his chair away and went for the door. I dropped some coins onto the table and followed him outside, and as we stood in the street he said, "Did you really think you could help me?"

"I don't know what I thought."

"You did, didn't you?"

I nodded.

"Help yourself, David," and he turned away and left me.

Maybe I should have followed him and pleaded with him to come back with me, or I could have pressed money into his hand, but I watched him walk away and disappear, and although I might have thought I had failed a friend, I did not.

I believe Timothy was a warning to me, and maybe he was right. He gave me a gift, a precious thing, one he could not open himself. We are all changed, some by events, others by our own nature, others by force of will. You choose your course, and only you can save yourself. No God, no words, no actress, no dance. It is not easy to alter fate, but it is possible. Once he had told me he was going to do good in the world, and maybe he would. And as I walked away from Exmouth Market and took the streets back to Highbury, I felt a new resolve come down upon me, like a spirit from heaven, or whatever paradise sparkled in the grey of the city and my slowly blooming mind.

In the afternoon, I called on William at St Bartholomew's Hospital. He said he had been trying to find me. Where had I been? What had I be doing? I did not say, but I did say that he did not have to do any more work on the stuff I had given him. The time had passed.

"You're as mysterious as this," he said, taking the phial from a glass cabinet, holding it to the light, shaking it and putting it on his desk. "Where did you get it?"

"It's a long story. Too long."

"Are you going to tell me?"

"Not today."

"Why not?"

"Because it's complicated. And you wouldn't believe me."

"I don't think so."

"Later," I said.

"I think you should tell me."

"I can't. Not yet, anyway."

"Well..." he said, and he picked up the phial again and squinted at it. "It's the strangest stuff I've ever seen, and

I've seen some strange stuff." He opened a drawer and pulled out a sheaf of notes. "I won't confuse you – God knows I'm confused enough myself – but so far I've found a number of acids, irons" – he paused and shuffled some notes – "and a range of vitamins. These are easy to identify, but there are other things in there. Strange, unusual solutions. I found traces of Lubritol, and that gave me a clue…"

"What's Lubritol?"

"Well…"

"Tell me."

He looked at me and scratched his chin. "I assume you know what metastasis is?"

"Yes."

"Then put two and two together."

"And get what?"

"I don't know. It's not responding to any of the standard tests. Clues, hunches, they're one thing. Empirical truth, that's what I need."

"William?"

I think he anticipated my question and interrupted before I could ask it. "I'm sorry," he said, "but I'm a scientist, David. I'll need a few more days, but I can't guarantee anything. As I said, it's strange stuff." He shuffled his notes again. "Can I ask; why does your friend take it?"

"She had a skin complaint."

"Had?"

"Yes."

"So she doesn't have it any more?"

"No."

"It cleared up on its own?"

"You could say that."

"Meaning?"

"Meaning…" I said, but I could not finish the sentence. The words stuck in my throat like thorns, the memories shattered and scattered, and when I looked at the floor I thought I could see them flapping at my feet like stranded fish. I stood up. "Thank you for your work, William. Keep it," I said, pointing at the phial, "if you want."

"Well…" And now he gave me a look of the deepest concern and said, "You know, David, if you want to talk about this, I'd be happy to listen. More than happy."

"I don't think happy comes into it."

"I'm sorry," he said, "I didn't mean to say the wrong thing."

"You didn't," I said, and I took a ten-pound note from my pocket and put it on his desk, and before he could say anything else I said, "For your trouble."

"That's very generous…"

"Give it to your orphans," I said, and an hour later I was on a railway train, travelling away from the city, a bag on the luggage rack and my eyes closed against the world.

The fields and orchards were being harvested, and the smell of apples and hops filled the air. When I reached Canterbury, my father was waiting for me. We sat in his sitting room and watched the river beneath the window, talked about the books he had been reading, and when he went to the kitchen to make a pot of tea, he asked me what I had been doing. I told him about Ashbrittle and the Buff-Orpington collection, and I told him I had visited Norfolk, but I said nothing about Isabel. Then he said, "Would you like to hear my news?"

"Yes please."

"It might surprise you." His eyebrows went up and a twinkle appeared in his left eye.

"Please, Father," I said. "Surprise me," expecting him to tell me he was learning German.

"I've taken up archery."

I laughed. "You, Father? Bows and arrows?"

"Yes, David. Me."

"And to think," I said, "you used to hate games. You used to say they were the Devil's work."

"There are games and there are games," he said, "and archery is different."

"How?"

He smiled, and his grey, drawn face was lighter than I had ever seen it. "Because it's more than a game. It's a battle with someone else and yourself, and it's a punishment that can give you such a feeling of joy. When you draw the string and feel the bow strain, and the arrow flies away from you..." His eyes rolled back and he looked at the ceiling before looking back at me. "Yes. It's more than a game. And of course, you meet so many interesting people."

"Good Lord!" I said, and then I stopped myself. When I was a child, using the creator's name as an exclamation would have led to a severe punishment, but now he smiled as he poured the tea and asked me if I was courting. I was surprised again – he had never asked such a personal question – so I said I was seeing someone, and although we had only known each other for a few weeks we had already been through a great deal together.

"When can I meet her?"

"I don't know, father."

"And where does she live?"

"Dorset."

"Ah, Dorset. What a beautiful county. Sometimes I wonder if I should have moved to Dorset." He smiled at the thought. "Anywhere we know?"

"Charmouth."

"That's on the coast, isn't it?"

"Yes."

"And what does she do?"

"She was an assistant to a scientist."

"She must be very clever."

"She was," I said. "She was very clever."

"Was?"

"Is, I mean," I said, but before he could ask me where we met or what our plans were, I changed the subject and told him I was thinking about resigning from Mitchell's but did not know what I wanted to do next.

"But I thought you loved your work."

"I used to."

"So what has happened?"

"Things."

"What kind of things, David? Explain."

I shook my head. "I can't. Not yet, anyway."

"But you will tell me when you're ready?"

"Of course, Father."

"Good," he said, and he poured the tea.

I had planned to take the train to Salisbury and stay the night in a hotel, but when my father suggested I stay with him I said I would. "Good boy," he said. "This definitely calls for a glass of whisky."

"You drink whisky?"

"Yes."

I shook my head. "What else do you do now?"

"Ah..." he said, and he tapped the side of his nose. "We shall not all sleep..."

"Of course," I said.

"Yes. Whisky and archery," and he pulled out two glasses and a bottle of Glenturret. "Do you remember Crieff?"

How could I forget Crieff? A holiday when I was about nine, a year before my mother died. We stayed in the Hydro, and spent the time walking the hills between the lowlands and the highlands.

If smell is the closest sense to memory, then my memories of Scotland are pine forests, wet grass and the distillery by a river, the woods and a bubbling stream. A famous cat lived there, and the smell of the stills and barrels and barley clung to my nostrils, and my mother's dress blew around my face as I stood and listened to a woman talk about the water of life, and as we walked home Father explained that the true water of life came from God, and the ground was wet and the trees dripped.

"I never realized," he said, "that in moderation this could be such a fine drink." He held the bottle up to the light, poured two glasses, raised his to mine and we drank until the sun went down and a cold wind picked up, blew down the river and rattled the windows

We talked about things we had never talked about before – school, work, my mother, disappointments – but when his eyes started to droop and I started to feel a green mist in my blood, I said it was time for bed, and he agreed. As we stood at the bottom of the stairs, he reached out, patted my shoulder and said he was proud of me and the things I had done. Then he leant towards me and kissed my forehead. I had never felt his lips before, and as they touched my skin, I felt a flutter in my heart, the tremble of love. I think I had always loved him in the way a son loves his father, but this was different, unconditional and ready to battle.

"Father..." I said, but that is all I could say.

"It's a miracle," he slurred, and although I did not ask why he thought it was, I knew why I thought it was. And when I lay down to sleep on the day bed, tucked up with a blanket, my memories became my dreams.

* * *

In the morning, I said goodbye to my father at his door and promised to see him the following month. We hesitated, but we put our arms around each other before parting, and then I walked the mile to the station and caught the train to Salisbury. I stopped in the old town to eat a pie and look at the cathedral. As I sat and ate, the flat noon light tried to diminish the stone, and I watched some masons working on the roof of the building. They were carrying sacks of tools, and stopped when they reached a corner. One of them pointed to a line of carvings and shouted something to the others. His voice carried to where I was sitting, but I did not hear what he said. I watched them for ten more minutes, the light failed and I walked back through the town. I stopped to look in a few shop windows, but I did not go in the second-hand bookshop I passed. I did not even give the dog-eared books in boxes a second look. Some old habits might die hard, but others have unexpected heart attacks and drop dead in old English cathedral cities, and even if you wanted to, there is nothing you can do about it. Habits cannot lose weight and they do not exercise, and they always spend too much time lying around with their feet up, smoking.

I hired a gig, took the Shaftesbury road and stopped at the top of the drive to my old school. Term had not started, and the playing fields were green and pure. The buildings were quiet and closed. The leaves on the trees were turning. I remembered the corridors, the classrooms and Russeter. The drive wound away in front of me, twisting and turning like it had always done, and I thought of how I had walked that drive and wondered how life would turn out.

I drove on, through Dorset, over the hills and the glimpses of ocean until I saw the first signs for Charmouth. When I reached the village, I left the gig with a boy who said he loved horses and walked down to the sea. I stood and watched people walking along the beach, heads down, looking for fossils. I shivered at the sea, turned and headed back the way I had come.

The house was at the top of the main street. I stood on the opposite side of the road and stared at its windows for a minute before crossing and knocking on the door. It was answered by a small woman who was exactly as I had imagined Isabel's mother would look, except she was wearing glasses. She said, "Yes?"

"I'm David," I said. "David Morris."

"Ah," she said. "Isabel's friend."

"That's right."

"How nice to meet you."

"Is she at home?"

"Yes. She's upstairs." She turned and shouted, "Isabel!" then turned back to me and said, "Do come in."

I stepped inside and was shown into a large sitting room. There were pictures on the walls and the smell of baking in the air. A moment later, Isabel appeared. She smiled at me, and I knew I had not been wrong. I kissed her hand and she said, "Would you like to see the garden?"

"Yes please."

We walked down the hall, past rows of pictures of famous people and beautiful places, and out through the back door. The garden was surrounded by high walls, and three steps led up to a small lawn. There was a small wooden bench there, a mimosa tree and climbing plants. We sat down. I saw her mother through the kitchen window. She was putting the kettle on the stove. I adjusted my laces and said, "So, how are you?"

"Getting better every day." She looked at the grass. "I was sick for a couple of weeks. Tired, listless, I couldn't do much, but I'm fine now. Almost back to normal." She pulled up her sleeve and showed me her arm. "Look."

The skin was clear and white, and although there was a patch of roughness near her elbow, the rest was smooth.

"Wonderful," I said, stupidly. I felt awkward, like I was the first man who had ever sat with her in this lovely place. "And your mother seems very nice."

"She is very nice."

We stared at each other, and I think we were thinking about the same things. I started with "When you left…" but did not know how to finish the sentence, so I left it there and listened while she told me an investigator had visited her and asked her if she knew a Professor Hunt, formally of Cambridge, who had disappeared from his rooms and had not been seen for over six months. She said she had told them she had been his assistant, but had not seen him for over a year, and she asked them if they had any idea where he was, and they had said, "He appears to have gone slightly mad, but no one we've spoken to has shown any sympathy for the man. In some cases, people have actually smiled at the news, and that's normally the last thing you expect in these circumstances."

I nodded at the news, but did not say anything, and when she thought about it she did not say any more either.

"And how is Charmouth?"

"Quiet. Quiet, but I like it."

"What did you tell your parents?"

She shrugged. "I just embellished the lie I wrote in the letter I sent about Scotland. I told them I was working on a dig in Helmsdale, looking for fossilized corals."

"Why didn't you tell them the truth?"

"How could they believe the truth?"

Her hair was starting to grow back, and her face was beautiful. The skin looked polished, and her eyes were shiny brown, like fresh conkers. I reached out and took her hand, put it to my lips, kissed it and let go. It left a vague scent in the air, like a passage. "Have you been fossiling here?"

"Yes. Most days. I found a fish yesterday." She went indoors, came back with it and showed it to me. She unwrapped it and said, "I've got some more work to do on it, but you can see its head, its back..." She licked her fingers and rubbed its grey scales. It was about the size of a plaice, and its mouth was curled up in what could have been a fish smile. I touched its dead eye and then we had one of those silences where the air turns heavy with expectation. I waited, she waited and we waited together, and then she said, "I love this garden." She moved her hand towards mine, hesitated, took it and smiled. "It's where I had my earliest memory."

"What was it?"

"I had a kitten. He was called Max. He wasn't very strong, he never had been, and one day he just faded away and died. I buried him over there." She pointed to a pile of stones in the corner of the garden. "I was about four, and I remember lying in bed thinking that Max would grow into a tree and there'd be kittens on the tree. And when I fell asleep, I dreamt about the tree and that all the kittens were hanging from the branches by their tails, wanting me to pick them."

"Good Heavens."

"I know. Some of the kittens were black and some of them were tabbies, and the one at the top was ginger. They were wriggling and crying, and a few of them fell down and ran away."

"And did you have one?"

"I don't know. I think I woke up before I had the chance." She reached down, picked up a fallen leaf, rolled it between her fingers and said, "What's your earliest memory?"

I remembered walking down the road to church with my mother, my hand in hers, the smell of her best coat wafting around me and my trousers scratching my legs. I do not know if this was earlier than one I had about picking some snowdrops and carrying them into the kitchen and being told

I was a kind boy. I said, "I'm not sure. You'll have to ask me another day."

"All right," she said.

We sat in silence for five minutes, and the wind started to blow. Her mother came out and asked if we wanted a cup of tea and a biscuit. We said we would, but before we went inside I said, "And you're well?"

"Yes, David. Every day in every way..."

"What about the rest of your life?"

"What about it?"

"Is it back to normal?"

"It could be," she said.

"Could be?"

"Should be," she said, and she held my hand. She lifted it to her mouth, kissed it and I kissed her, and when she smiled I thought back to the last time I had seen her, and how she had left me in Norfolk in the early morning with a half-burnt candle on the window sill and the smell of creosote in the air.

I thought back to the time when the dawn snapped and lines of light dripped into the dark. When I straightened her arms and legs, washed the blood from her scales, removed the pillow from the bed and spread a fresh sheet over her. Here, when I kneeled and bowed my head so it touched her fingers, and I reached across her body and stroked her face. And here, I picked a strand of cotton from the top of her head. Then I stood up, blew out the candles and stood by the door. I looked at her and wished, but nothing happened. For a moment, even the marshes were silent, and the birds still. The curtains hung down and dust settled. I left her alone in the dark.

I walked through the marshes. The light was milky and blue and pale together. I could feel the way. It was flat. I heard the reeds, and the sea came washing in after the storm. It came like a bride to the altar, arm in arm with the sky, breaking with a sigh, sinking slowly.

When I reached the beach I walked towards the place where we had flown the kite and looked for it, but did not see it.

I sat down and stared at the waves as the sun rose through a low hedge of cloud and light exploded across the sea. I blinked and shaded my eyes, and birds rose behind me and flew away. For a moment I wished I could make a sandcastle, a tall one with turrets, a moat and paper flags. I wanted to wait and count the minutes until the tide came in. So many wants, so many coulds. I could go for a long walk through the Americas. I could do good in a poor country. Or I could do exactly the same things I have always done, make no plans, work each day, sleep more than I should, and wait.

I sat, and as the sun climbed, tiredness crept up and flooded my body. I stood up, turned my back on the sea and walked away, and when I reached the marshes I did not stop to listen to the bitterns as they crept through the reeds.

When I reached my house and opened the door, silence seemed to blow out. I stepped inside and stood in the kitchen. The air still smelt faintly of the substance she had injected. I breathed it deeply, poured a glass of dark rum and sat down by the stove. I drank, leant back and closed my eyes.

Make no plans. Clear thought. Reason, not magic. You are responsible. You have choices and you can make them. Nothing means nothing else. Move across the land and empty your head. Have another drink. Do not worry about trying to work out what anything means. Give all unessential books to friends. Keep the good volumes in a box no bigger than a small horse can carry.

I was pouring another drink and thinking about boxes and what I would do with her body. Should I take it to the beach and burn it below the tide line, or steal a boat and burn it at sea? I was thinking in faster and faster circles when I heard a sound. It was sharp, like a door frame snapping, followed by a thud and a moan. I jumped up. I hit the table with my knee and the rum flew across the room. I heard the moan again. It came from behind me, from the bedroom. There was heavy breathing, feet banging against the walls and another sound, like paper tearing. I ran through and found Isabel on the floor between the bed and the wall. She was lying on her stomach. Her skin had split down the centre of her back and was hanging off her like cloth. The scales had lost their colour and turned translucent, her real skin was shining beneath a film of blood and other fluid. She was shivering all over and making little whining noises, like mice trapped in bottles.

I turned her over, and as I did she groaned from the back of her throat, opened her eyes and smiled at me.

"Isabel?"

"Ah…"

"Isabel!" I pulled her up. "What's happening?"

"I…" She concentrated, her eyes screwed tight shut, and as her lips moved, some scales rubbed onto my trousers.

"Breathe," I said, uselessly.

"I'm…'

"You're?"

"I'm moult…" she reached up and grabbed her shoulder.

"You're moulting?"

"Yes," and she nodded and started tugging at a hole in the skin. It was the size of a coin. She stuck her finger in and pulled gently. As she did, she winced and buckled, but did not stop. The skin crackled, and as it came away, dead scales flaked like confetti. They drifted in the air as she worked her way to her elbow, tugged, and the whole piece dropped off and lay on the floor.

"You need anything?"

She nodded, pointed to her mouth and licked her lips.

I fetched two glasses of water, and when I got back to her she was sitting on the bed, the whole of her back was clear of scales and she was pulling them off her head. She moaned as she peeled them away from her eyes and ears, and wiped the blood and pus away. "Ah…" she said, and she dropped them on the floor, took the glass of water from me and drank it in one gulp. "Tha… thanks…"

"More?"

She nodded.

I poured as she put her fingers underneath the rip beneath her chin and started to pull. Now she became shy, turned and waved me away. The snake skin was hanging over her breasts and, where she had stretched, a broken line appeared along her waist, like a huge laugh. I could see her navel.

"I'll be in the kitchen," I said. "Call if you need me," and I left her.

I do not know how long I sat by the sink and stared at the marshes. It was probably about half an hour. I knew she had finished when she yelled and the house was quiet for a moment. Then she laughed and opened the bedroom door. Before I had a chance to turn and look at her she was in the bathroom, the door locked, and she laughed again. She started to wash and sing. I have no idea what song it was, but it went up and down. I fetched a fresh towel and waited for her to come out, and when I saw her I held it up for her and said "It's clean."

She whispered, "Clean…"

"Yes, Isabel."

"Thank you."

"You're welcome."

"And I'm clean…" she said, and she twisted herself into the towel, came to the kitchen and sat down. "I'm clean!"

"I can see."

"Very clean!"

"You look fine…"

"I feel…" she started, but then she stopped.

"What happened?"

She shook her head and stared at me for a minute. Then another minute and another before she said, "I heard you leave. I heard everything but I couldn't do anything about it. I was lying in there and I think I fell asleep. I don't know how long I slept, but when I woke up I felt almost well. For a moment I thought I was dreaming or dead, and when I looked, there was a split on my arm. Here…" She touched the place. "And when I pushed my finger in, it started to come away…"

"Amazing…"

"And I remember something Hunt told me, something about how one day I'd moult, and when that happened it could make or break the experiment. I had to grow fresh skin or else it was a failure."

"It was a failure."

"I think you're right," she said, and she rubbed a place where the snake skin had left a mark. "I know you're right," and then I fetched a couple of clean glasses, poured some rum and we started to drink. We drank until the glasses were empty, and when I suggested more she said, "Yes please," so we carried on. The more she drank the more she stared and stroked her skin, and by the time we were ready for bed, dawn was cracking over the house. "Strange days," she said, and

I agreed, but I was too tired to think. I lay back, closed my eyes and let the old day fold around me, like a towel your mother holds out as you climb out of the bath and you are polished with water.

She stayed with me in Norfolk for a couple of days and then I took her to Norwich. She was going home to Dorset. I offered to travel with her, but she said she could manage, she was a grown woman. And she said she wanted to spend some time on her own, she wanted to think, sleep, read and sleep. So I kissed her on the cheek and left her on the railway-station platform, promised to see her soon, rode back to my place and sat on the veranda. When it started to drizzle, I carried my chair to the garden, sat by the statue of the dog and let the rain soak me. I did not feel the cold and did not feel the wind against my face, and I did not notice as the evening crept up and wrapped its arms around me. One more evening and one more night, and all the things I had thought came back and wished themselves into my head.

I took stock and realized it was true. I did not want to be a book valuer any more. I wanted to tie my mind with twine and put it in a small box for a year, then take it out and pretend the last few months had not happened. I wanted to see my father and walk through the back streets of Canterbury with him, and I wanted to see Isabel again, Isabel with her own skin and her own hair. I fetched some paper and a pen, sat at the table and started to write. I wrote for an hour, then got up and did some tidying around the house. I found a blouse under the bed. It was Isabel's, and when I held it to my nose her smell came back to me. It came in floods, and was easy enough – and later, after I had written ten pages, I took the blouse to bed with me and slept with my face to the window.

Epilogue

I wrote this story in my low house at the bottom of a small garden. Turn your back on the marshes, cross the lawn, go past the trees and flowers, and the pond with the reeds and frogs.

The house sits on bricks and used sleepers. Climb some steps, watch out for a loose board and cross a veranda to get inside, and there you are, standing with the light pooling on the floor and the sound of birds singing in the marshes.

The place has got a bedroom at the back, a sitting room and kitchen in front and a small bathroom. The walls are made of cedar with a felted pitched roof, two windows at the front, the door in the middle and two windows in the sides and back.

The air smells of ripening apples, ink, a stuffed deer's head someone bought, put in a wardrobe and forgot about. It has its own memories, of visitors and spilt tea and oil lamps burning on the sterns of sinking ships, and lost days. I say it has these memories, but I cannot tell what is hidden beneath the solid floors, or what the blank windows have seen.

I have some painted furniture, carpets and rugs, pictures of castles on cliffs and a stove in the corner of the sitting room. There is a table in the kitchen and in a cupboard a telescope that does not work. Three chairs that do not match, a bowl of fruit and some porridge crusted onto a bowl. A pepper mill and a note on the wall that reads "Please close down the stove before leaving". A melted candle, some white pebbles we found on the beach, and puddles of hard wax on the sill. All the curtains have shrunk, so there is a gap around the bottom of the windows.

When the wind blows the house moans, and when the sun shines it creaks, and when it rains it sighs like it wants the rain so much, and now here it is and here I am, listening all the time.

Now I have finishing writing this story, I have decided to get away and do something I have never done before. With this in mind, I was going to read a book about a man who travelled through Asia to visit his Aunt. I read the first page. The man was standing outside a hotel in Glasgow, he had lost his pen and it was raining. I did not read any more.

I did not read any more because here you can sit at the kitchen table, dab your fingers in a pool of spilt milk and look out at the garden. Or you can lie in bed and not read a book and listen to the curlews, or you can walk up the garden path, through the gate, across the road and into the marshes.

The marshes whisper and the marshes cry and the marshes threaten. They are like someone you like but cannot trust. They never look you in the eye and they never offer to pay their share. They whisper behind their hands and walk with a sloping grin. If you leave the paths, the ground will look fine but will lead into a swamp and you will slip and fall and either spend your last night on earth face down in water or face up, and birds will eat your eyes. Some people say, "The marshes are so beautiful and lonely..." and they are right, but they do not know the whole story. It is too easy to say those sort of things about a place, as though beauty can hide a grave.

So this is my house at the edge of the marshes with its roof, windows and tables, and there go a flock of geese and this is my house too. It is like everyone's other house, a place where mysteries, promises, dreams and terrors are kept.

It is not a lasting state, this house, but it changes every day. It holds things that never leave – the memory of the first time I saw Isabel, the sound of her cries echoing through the night, the smell of sweat and salt, the feel of her – and it grows, twists and adds things to itself.

It could be mad or it could be angry, or it could double back on itself and become taller than the tallest building in a city. It could be yellow and black and talk in a language only it understands. It could whisper about careless times, or flare like a candle and become the person you loved. Her name could chime. It could be Isabel or Grace or someone else, someone whose name you cannot say any more, but when you are so lonely and you pull her picture from an envelope and stare at it in the middle of the night you know she was the love of your life and you will never forget her. You can smell her skin, but then the smell fades and passes. It has gone, and before you have a chance, you find yourself screaming in the night and wailing into the day.

It is as bad as that, as bad as the grave-digger who thinks, for a second, about what would happen if the man at the top walked away and left him there with his spade, rope and bucket and the block of light shining down. Or it could be a pale sky and we are walking along, and skylarks are watering the air with their songs. The sky is the roof and the larks are bees in the rafters, and I wake in the late afternoon from a dream about being a more dangerous man than I am.

I sit up and as the wind plays with the marshes, I remember how her skin used to ripple like water under ice. I used to lean towards her, put my ear next to her nose and listen to her breathing. I used to do these things, but I am different now, changed. I do not imagine I am clever, and I do not think I am pleased. When I remember things I have done and people I have known, I realize I was never true to them or true to myself. I spent too much time lost between what I thought made me happy and the ideas of happiness that were fed to me. But happiness only comes when you stop playing games and realize the only thing you have is your state of mind. This is all there is, nothing more. And at the moment my state of mind is quiet and I feel like the air in an empty drawer, scented with old possessions and old hands. I can see myself fresh and still, and I sit without wondering or waiting, and I listen to the wind as dust balls roll around my feet.

I read as I wait, then get up and stand at the window. I suppose I should go outside and do some work in the garden, but I will not. The beds and borders do not interest me and the lawn can grow as tall as a forest. I am not tired but I want to sleep, but I only want to sleep if Isabel is beside me. I want to listen to her beating heart and smell her skin. I want to close my eyes and feel her lips on my face. I want to hear her voice whispering in my ear.

But this is not going to happen yet. I am dreaming, turning like a falling leaf in whispering air. I say I am dreaming, but Isabel did come back, she did visit me here again, in the spring, as she travelled on her way to London. She had determined to become a nurse, and was to begin work at St Thomas's Hospital. When she arrived, I made her a cup of tea and offered her a plate of small cakes, and as we sat on the veranda and I listened to her talk about her plans, it came to me. I say it came to me, but I suppose it was with me all the time, for how could it not have been? How could something so simple have gone unnoticed? For as she had shed her skin, so I had shed my fears and memories, and all the things that had bound me to the top floor of life. They had flown south like swallows, caught the warm air, and I told her this. "There is change in everything," I said. "Change is the engine of the world."

"Yes," she said. "Maybe it is."

"It is," I said. "All my life I thought I should live one way, without thinking there are many ways. A thousand ways. I was foolish, blind and foolish."

"No," she said. "You were never foolish."

"I was."

She smiled now and nodded, but she was not going to argue. So for another moment we sat and listened as the late birds flew home, a small wind blew, and the garden gate squeaked on its hinges.

"What were your fears?" she said.

"Many."

"Name me one."

"That I would never do anything worthwhile. That I would always do mundane work in a safe world."

"Now you are fooling yourself."

"Am I?"

"Why?"

"You know why."

"Tell me."

"You saved me, David, and that was far from mundane."

"I thought…"

"Thought what?"

"That maybe… maybe I would never be able to love. Or find…" I stopped the words in my throat for a moment. "Someone who needs me. Loves me."

She reached out and took my hand, held it in hers and stroked it. I looked at her skin. It was pale and smooth, and beautiful. I remembered how she used to look, her face and back and neck, and I said, "Do you remember? How you used to be?"

"Of course."

"And what do you think now?"

"I think I have another life. And I think I'm grateful."

Now I wanted to weep, to tell her that if I had a chance I would want to love her and have her love me, but at that time I knew it was useless. There was only so much change in time. She was bound to the ambition to do good in a greater world than I knew, and sweep like a ship across an ocean I would never sail. I would stay in the marshes with the birds and the sky.

"You have to leave things behind," she said. "You have to know how to say goodbye."

"I suppose so."

"You do know how to love."

"You think so?"

"I know you do."

"Sometimes I doubt it. Sometimes I think love is just a cupboard your mind hides inside."

"That's not a good way to think," she said, "not a good way at all. And it's not true."

"I know, but I don't think like that all the time. Sometimes I think that all I have to do is learn patience."

"Maybe," she said, and now I held my breath, "maybe one day I'll teach you."

"Would you?"

"Yes," she said, "of course I will. Did you ever doubt it?" and she leant towards me, took my chin in her hand and kissed my cheek. Her lips felt like nothing at all, and she smelt of lemon. Lemon, a perfect fruit. Light, sour and fresh. Waiting. "Learn patience, David," and as her words hung in the air, I thought she was going to tell me something else, something I wanted to hear. I almost prayed for it, but what is prayer to the faithless? On the other hand, what is prayer with faith? How can the divine help when the divine is such a failing lie? In either case, if an answer is heard, the answer is only made of empty words bred by imagination, words with no more power than a skipping rhyme. I would have to wait for my mind to clear, for our desires to meet and coalesce, and for the clouds to part. And waiting was something I had never done before, not properly, not carefully. And like the doubting apostle who placed his hand in the wounds and felt the scales drop from his eyes, so I knew that one day Isabel and I would walk back to this place, and I would meet her again where the stabbing bitterns court, wet or dry, dead or alive. There was no doubt, no doubt at all. And as she left and closed the gate, I watched her hair and the fainting rain, opened my mouth to call but let the words stop in my mouth, and I turned back to this, my pen and the ancient Pauline truth.

BORN IN 1956, PETER BENSON WAS EDUCATED IN Ramsgate, Canterbury and Exeter. His first novel, *The Levels*, won the Guardian Fiction Prize. This was followed by *A Lesser Dependency*, winner of the Encore award, and *The Other Occupant*, which was awarded the Somerset Maugham Award. He has also published short stories, screenplays and poetry. His work has been adapted for TV and radio, and his novels are translated around the world.

www.almabooks.com